Madigan's Lady

When the call came for Chief U.S. Marshal Parminter to help stop a spate of bank robberies and bloody killings, there was only one man to send – 'Bronco' Madigan.

That was fine with Madigan, even though he felt his confidence slipping a little. He was getting old and too many old wounds were slowing him down. So, signing on as bronc-buster for Colonel Bodine's Wild West Show, sounded like a good deal. Something different, something easier. . . .

But he was wrong. From the moment he arrived, bullets and fists flew thick and fast until the final showdown tested him to the limit. Now it was a case of still being up to the job – or dying a painful death.

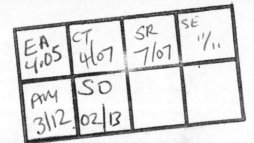

Madigan's Lady

HANK J. KIRBY

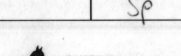

A Black Horse Western

ROBERT HALE · LONDON

ISBN 0 7090 7364 X

Robert Hale Limited
Clerkenwell House
Clerkenwell Green
London EC1R 0HT

Typeset by
Derek Doyle & Associates, Liverpool.
Printed and bound in Great Britain by
Antony Rowe Limited, Wiltshire

CHAPTER 1

THE RAIN MEN

Mrs Chapman, the banker's wife, opened the door to find a smiling young man standing in the rain on the stoop, not yet stepping up on to the porch.

It was only half-light because it was a bleak Sunday afternoon and the rain was heavy. It splashed off his neck-to-toes slicker; his head was buried deep, hat pulled down low. He touched a hand to the brim and water poured off the stiff felt.

'Sorry, ma'am, trying not to make a mess of your porch.' He glanced around. 'This is a right fine house, ain't it?'

The compliment pleased her and she nodded, giving him a half-smile, but as lunch was on the table and the family were awaiting her presence, she said rather abruptly, 'What can I do for you, young man?'

'Well, ma'am, it's really Mr Chapman I need to see.' He placed one muddy boot on the edge of the porch, bending his leg a little, leaning forward in a

5

conspiratorial manner. 'Urgent message for him from the sheriff.'

'Sheriff Ewbanks?' she said a little stupidly, now feeling a little lurch in her stomach; any message from the lawman wasn't likely to be anything social, even on a Sunday afternoon. She stood aside, holding open the door a little more. 'You'd best come in.'

She was disappointed when he did so and failed to remove his hat, although she looked at it pointedly. He smiled again, a nice friendly smile. Then he grabbed her by the upper arm so tightly that she gave a small involuntary cry, began to struggle.

She sucked in a gasping, shuddering breath as a gun barrel butted brutally against her ribs and she was dragged towards the lamplight spilling out of the dining-room; it was dark enough in the house to need artificial light.

'Let's go meet the rest of the family, ma'am.'

They were waiting patiently at the table, which was set formally with plate, knife, fork and dessert spoon in four places, one in front of a young girl about sixteen, beginning to blossom, with that innocence of childhood just starting to disappear and a knowing look in her eyes when she looked at agreeable young men these days; beside her sat a smaller girl, with similar features but with darker hair, about twelve years old and freckled. Richard Chapman, the banker, sat at the head of the table, erect, lord of the manor, in a tailored grey frockcoat, showing a silk vest-front over a white shirt with a knotted string bow tie: clothes he had worn to church earlier in the day. He was a man in his forties, well-fed, well-bred, possibly, and now the look of patient curiosity that had been on his quite handsome face ever since his wife had gone to answer the inconvenient knock on the front door, suddenly disappeared and he lunged to his feet, face darkening.

'What the devil is this!' he demanded and the gun swung to cover him, gestured jerkily.

'Sit down quietly, sir, and you'll find out.'

'I'll damn well find out right now!' He started around the table, fists knotting. 'This is my house and that's my wife's arm you're holding! If you don't release her this instant . . .'

That was as far as he got.

The intruder's gun swung in a short arc, cracked dully against Mrs Chapman's head and she slumped, blood trickling from beneath her hairline. The little girl screamed and the older one gasped, going white, a hand reaching to cover her mouth as her eyes widened.

Richard Chapman stopped cold in his tracks, jaw sagging as the man let his wife fall to the floor in an inert heap. The gun barrel swung to cover her huddled body.

'One more step, sir, and I'll shoot her.'

'My God! This is – this is outrageous! Who d'you think you—'

'I'm just a feller in need of a little help, Mr Chapman. Now, *sit down, damn you!*'

Chapman was so shocked – couldn't take his eyes off his unconscious wife – that he backed up to his chair and dropped into it.

'Daddy!' said the sixteen-year-old girl in a tiny

voice, reaching out for his hand.

He covered it quickly with one of his, patted it with the other. 'It's all right, Bunty, it's all right – I'll find out what this young man wants and then he'll leave us alone.' He raised pleading eyes to the intruder whose face was indistinct with shadows cast by his turned-up collar and the low hat-brim. 'Isn't that right. . . ?'

'It depends on how co-operative you are, banker.'

Chapman swallowed, getting his first inkling now of what this was all about.

'Don't harm my family! Please!'

The man made an innocent gesture with his hands.

'Not me, Mr Chapman – I won't hurt them – now that you seem to be reasonable. Point is, *how* reasonable are you going to be?'

'Anything! Anything you want – I'll co-operate.'

'Anything at all?'

Chapman hesitated, then took one look at his daughters and nodded jerkily. 'Whatever you want.'

'How about the keys to the bank vault. . . ?'

Richard Chapman was sweating under his long slicker although he felt a coldness inside, a shaky, nervous coldness. He glanced once more over his shoulder at the man who had knocked his wife unconscious as they made their way through the rain towards the bank. The streets were deserted, wet, muddy and miserable. Even the conscientious Sheriff Ewbanks was holed up in his office with a lantern throwing amber light around the small, stuffy room

8

as he read through his stack of old wanted dodgers. Refreshing his memory, for a lot of strangers passed through this town of Estralita.

'That – man who came to – watch my family,' the banker stammered, 'while you brought me here – I didn't much like the look of him. Mostly his voice – I didn't care for some of his remarks about my daughters.'

'He's OK – he knows what to do.'

Chapman took a chance, stopped dead at the foot of the steps that led to the bank's side door, turning to look straight at his captor. 'And just what does he have to *do?*'

'Watch your family. Turn them loose unharmed when he gets my signal.' The man hit him heavily on the shoulder now. Chapman staggered against the brick wall. 'Open up!'

Chapman fumbled at the keys, knowing he was in a real bind. This man knew to come to the side entrance, which couldn't be seen from Main Street. He knew there were two sets of keys for the door, but only one set for the vaults. He knew the names of all of Chapman's family – *and he knew that the accumulated payrolls for Fort Deacon and the Ralls Company Copper Mine were sitting in the vault!*

As the door opened Chapman turned swiftly to the right, hearing footsteps. His heart lifted, hoping it was Ewbanks making a patrol after all.

It wasn't. It was another tall, slicker-clad ranny coming down the narrow lane with a sawn-off shotgun in his hand, coming straight up to the man who held his sixgun on the banker.

'No trouble?'

'Had to put the lady to sleep to get this feller's attention, is all.'

The newcomer grunted, adjusted his high-crowned hat a little, poked at the nervous banker with the stubby barrels of the shotgun.

'Relax, banker. It ain't your money.'

'I – I'm responsible for it!'

The new man nodded. 'That's right. Which also makes you responsible for the safety of your family.'

The banker looked sharply at the first man. 'You said they'd be all right!'

'Up to you, though, ain't it? Now get in there, take the vault key from your hidey-hole and open them heavy doors.' He looked at his companion. 'Safe-maker reckons they'll stand the blast from twenty sticks of dynamite – even nitro, if you could drill a hole deep enough in that metal to pour some in.'

'Which is why we're doin' it this way,' the second man said with a growl in his voice. 'Let's get to it – I don't trust that Ewbanks. . . .'

Richard Chapman was almost weeping when he eventually opened the doors of the vault, then worked on the locks of the inner doors and swung them open.

The bank robbers whistled and grinned at each other when they saw the boxes and canvas sacks branded either US ARMY or RALLS COPPER COMPANY.

'Hope the greaser has his best pack-mules,' said the man who had first gone to the banker's house.

'He'll have plenty – and quit that "greaser" stuff,

will you? It's past a joke now an' he's working on a short fuse.'

'If he can't take a joke—'

The second man rammed the shotgun hard into the other's slicker, making him step back quickly, gasping a little. '*Cut it out!* Now call him up and start loading!'

The man didn't like it, that was plain enough, but he went to the side door, opened it about a foot and gave a soft whistle, rubbing at his lower ribs under the stiff slicker material. The look he threw the other man was bleak as the weather that was now hammering on the shingles, making it necessary for them to raise their voices.

'He's coming. Got both mules.'

The man with the shotgun jerked the barrels at Chapman, making the man step back, half-raising his hands.

'Told you to relax. We ain't finished with you. You can help load.'

Chapman seemed as if he would protest but then a third man entered, water streaming from his poncho, face mostly hidden by the shadow of his wide-brimmed hat. He rubbed his hands together.

'Aiy-aiy-yieee! Looka dat loot, eh, *amigo?*'

The shotgun man glanced at the other tall one who arched his eyebrows.

'That don't sound like greaser talk to you?'

'Move!'

The shotgunner stood by and watched the three of them take out the boxes and sacks and load them on to the pack mules waiting in the alley. Chapman was breathing heavily with only a little exertion, clutched at his chest several times, began to complain about pains, but the shotgun clipped him on the head and, dazed, he staggered back to the vault, took one more sack and started back.

The shotgun pressed into his belly. 'Take two.'

'I – I – can't manage two. Feel – queer . . . Pains . . .'

'We just about finish, *jefe*,' said the short man in the big hat, half-lifting it, showing most of his face briefly, a stiff smile also visible.

'OK,' said the shotgunner and pulled one trigger.

The blast hurled Chapman half-way into the vault. His body shook the shelf and a bag of coins burst, spilling a silver cascade on to the floor. The other two men jumped, shocked.

'Judas priest!' gasped the tall man, staring at the shotgunner. 'Why'd you. . . ?'

'Because of you two!' the man snapped, pushing a fresh shell into the barrel he had fired. There was cold anger in his voice. 'One of you mentions a name that might mean something, the other shows his goddamn face, puts on a stupid accent – didn't we plan it better'n this!'

The two men were silent, picked up the last of the money sacks and carried them to the waiting mules. The shotgunner hustled them out, closed the side door behind him and locked it.

The short man was already leading the mules down to the far end of the lane. The others turned back towards Main and the shotgunner said:

'Back to the banker's place.'

The other stopped. 'We don't have to go there.

When we ride past, Utah'll know it's OK . . .'

'We don't leave witnesses behind now, not with the banker dead.'

'Christ! There're two young girls . . .'

'You want to risk spending time with 'em?'

'I didn't mean that. They're just – kids!'

'And we're big bad robbers – or s'posed to be! You two fouled it up. Now you go in there with Utah and tie up the loose ends.'

'Not me! I—'

The shotgun bruised his ribs and he looked into the cold face of the other.

'I don't mind a bigger share,' the man said, cocking the shotgun's hammers.

The other man sighed and nodded, started towards the banker's house.

'Wait up, you two!'

The voice came from behind them and they turned in time to see Sheriff Ewbanks stepping out of his office into the rain, right hand close to his sixgun.

'What're you doin' near the bank in this kinda weather? And was that a shot I heard above the rain?'

He started to draw his gun as he came forward, heedless of the rain drenching him. The two robbers fired together, the shotgun's roar drowning the crack of the six shooter. Ewbanks was flung back, going down to one knee, his gun hand half-burying the Colt in the mud as he tried to support himself, blood showing on his shirt-front, his head hanging. The robbers started to sprint towards the banker's house and Ewbanks reared up in one final effort, grasped his Colt in both hands. The gun wavered as he tried to line up his sights on the running men and then the life bubbled out of him. As he fell forward the Colt roared, jumping from his hands as he spread out in the slush.

He didn't see one of the slicker-clad figures lurch, stumble, almost go down, then come half-upright again and follow his companion who turned around, hurried back, gave him the support of one arm about his waist and led him away.

A dull crash of gunfire came from inside the banker's house and what might have been the beginning of a high-pitched scream, cut short.

CHAPTER 2

LAWMAN

When Madigan rode into the main street of Monroe, Colorado, he was leading a horse with two dead man roped across it, partly covered with a square of burlap. It was all he could find in the ruins of the old mine high up in the sierras.

They were good men now – because they were dead – but they had been bad sons of bitches before Madigan had caught up with them after following their trail of death and robbery for nigh on 500 miles. Quirt Rango – real name Herbert Millson – and self-styled Streak Norris.

They had terrorized the whole of Conway County for months, virtually doing what they liked, including killing any local lawman loco enough to go after them. By the time four sheriffs and three deputies were buried on various Boot Hills, folk had had enough and wrote the US marshal's office in Washington.

Send us someone fast with a gun who's not afraid to use it. . . .

Chief Marshal Miles Parminter had plenty of men who could fit the bill but the one he chose was Brendan 'Bronco' Madigan, his star lawman, who had been champing at the bit to break the shackles holding him to his desk after recovering from a bush-whacker's bullet in the back.

'We know who they are,' Parminter had told him, 'even know where they hang out – in general – which is the Sierra Constars, backing up to Conway County, the seat being at Monroe.'

'How come they haven't been flushed before this?' Madigan wanted to know.

'Bren, have you ever been to the Constars?' When the marshal shook his head, Parminter continued: 'Take a fishing line after you've hooked a big steel-eye bass that jumps all over the pool, burrows under rock ledges, bunches your line over, under and every whichway amongst the snags, and you've got some idea of what it's like in those sierras. The Spanish looked for silver there, found a little, so it's rumoured, but only one mule-load got out. The rest of the men and mules died in there somewhere – lost.'

'And these two soreheads, Rango and Norris, found a way in and out they could use whenever they felt like it?' Madigan sounded sceptical but Parminter, unsmiling as usual, nodded solemnly.

'They did, fazed every posse that went after them. Not only that, they holed up, bushwhacked them – and picked off every man wearing a star.'

Madigan shook his head. 'They must've been lucky. Neither one has enough brains to tie his shoelaces without help. I've spoken to whores who actually did it for 'em.'

Parminter frowned. *He* was the one to tell anecdotes here. 'Lucky or not, they're still in there and when they come out they scare the hell out of ordinary folk, rob and kill and rape. Time to end it, Bren.'

Madigan agreed, went down there to the Sierra Constars – which meant 'clear' or 'plain to see' in Spanish, and they were that, standing out like plywood cut-outs against the blue of a cloud-streaked Colorado sky. But they were also one hell of a tangled mess of gulches and draws and dead ends that would deter any posse, especially after the stories of lost dead men in there.

But Madigan didn't believe in ghosts and he searched until he found tracks. Hell, those two were so confident that they couldn't be found in here they didn't even bother to cover their trail in places. It took him five days and he not only located their hidey-hole in the ruins of the old Spanish silver-mine, he drew himself a map as he went so he could find his way out again.

The last job pulled by these two had involved the rape and murder of a family in the middle of a respectable town – the outlaws' way of thumbing their noses at the law in general. Madigan took that personally now that the case was his and he set himself up on a grey ridge of tailings that looked down on to the outlaws' campsite. They were well set up, near a spring, had built a crude shack and a sapling corral for their spare horses, but the place was a garbage dump of old food and wrappings and broken bottles, flies buzzing.

He waited patiently before sun-up and saw the first one come to the door of the cabin and urinate, swaying, only half-awake, some of his stream wetting his long johns. It didn't seem to bother him.

Then Madigan coolly drew a bead on him and a moment later nothing would ever bother Quirt Rango again.

The man crashed back into the cabin, fell with one leg protruding across the stoop. The rifle shot was echoing around the hills and as it died slowly Madigan heard the sounds from inside as the startled Streak Norris grabbed his guns.

'Who the hell *is* that?' he demanded hoarsely, not believing anyone had found the hideout.

'Madigan, US marshal. I don't intend to take you in alive, Streak. You want to make things easy, or have I got to come in after you?'

'Come ahead, you son of a bitch! If you think you'll live long enough to see the sun come up!'

A rifle barrel appeared in the only window-opening and three hurried shots raked the tailings pile. But Madigan knew that that opening was the only one the outlaw could use: he was already sighted on it. He triggered and levered twice, one shot tearing splinters from the ledge. Streak Norris reared back, swearing. The second bullet took him in the upper body and he went down hard.

Madigan didn't waste any time, knowing that the

man, if he was still alive, would expect him to wait a spell, then approach carefully. So Streak, bleeding from the chest but still with his wits about him, cried out in shock as Madigan appeared in the doorway of the cabin even before the wounded outlaw could bring his gun around to cover it.

Madigan put another bullet into his chest, then walked up and drove a third through his head.

He cooked breakfast, using his own grub and utensils, then loaded the bodies on one of the outlaws' own horses, turned loose the spare mounts and made his way out of the sierras and down to Monroe.

The town made a hero out of him although he tried his best to keep it low – a lot of publicity wasn't the best way to help a marshal who often had to go under cover. But folk came from miles around to shake the hand of the man who had finally rid them of the scourge of Rango and Streak.

They insisted on putting on a large barbecue and roasted an ox on the spit, trestle-tables groaning under the weight of home-made goodies. There were speeches and dancing and Madigan endured it all, knowing their intentions were good.

'Too bad the Wild West Show left town last week,' said the mayor, actually Bud Fleischner who ran the general store. 'We could've asked them to put on a special show for you, Marshal.'

Trying to be polite, but weary as hell and wanting to crawl into bed, Madigan asked: 'What wild west show is that, Bud?'

'Why, Captain Kerry Bodine's. You musta heard of it. Been travellin' all over for a couple years or more.'

'Only Kerry Bodine I know of was a sergeant kicked outta the army for misappropriation of funds – about five years back.'

The mayor frowned, shaking his head. 'Can't be the same man. This one is a hero of the Indian wars, wears the medals to prove it, and he has one of the best of that type of show this town has ever seen.'

'A medicine show? Hell, I've never seen a good one yet.'

'Hell, *no*! Not one of them snake-oil things where the main aim is to sell you all kinds of "miracle" crap. This is a rodeo and staged acts like an Indian attack on Fort Huachuca, only they call it "Fort Kerry" for the show – based on a real attack when Cap'n Bodine rode in with his troop and saved the whole shebang. They got sharp-shootin', Injun powwow dancin', even a stage set-up where actors do somethin' from what that limey poet or whatever he was wrote. Spearman?'

'Shakespeare. Well, I've been up north for a long time now. Never heard of "Captain" Bodine's show, but I might look it up if it's nearby . . .'

'Well, not exactly nearby. They play the bigger towns, see? Next one on their agenda was to be Grand Junction out near Orchard Lake, if you're goin' back that way.'

'Don't think so.'

'Well, you might catch 'em somewheres else. They're worth goin' outta the way for. They played Estralita a few weeks before comin' here, Santa Fe and Albuquerque before that – so they're on a kinda long swing through Colorado now.'

Madigan let the man ramble on, full of enthusiasm, and eventually managed to get away to bed.

When he left town the next day it was raining heavily but most folk lined the streets and cheered him on his way.

'*Ker-ist!*' he said to himself as he forced a smile and waved. '*Just what I need!*'

Madigan didn't return to Washington as his orders had stated.

He stopped at a town called Delta, at the junction of the Colorado and Gunnison Rivers, sold his horse – he liked to pick up a mount when he reached the town of his assignment for usually they were local and familiar with the type of country he would be working – and booked a passage on the riverboat south to Montrose. There a stagecoach would take him across the Wasatch Mountains and he would eventually reach Colorado Springs where he would pick up the first of a series of railroads on the long journey north.

It was mandatory that he checked in with US marshals' offices located in towns he would pass through.

At Montrose, he left the riverboat and booked into a cheap hotel for a night to await the stage that left in the morning for the Wasatch run.

He ate in the saloon bar across the street, had a couple of beers and bought some fresh tobacco and a long cigarillo to enjoy in his room with a quiet whiskey before turning in. He was damned weary and seemed to creak a little as he climbed the stairs to his room, top floor, back. His shoulder ached near the spot where the bushwhacker's bullet had hit him and the doctor had told him he was lucky to pull through.

'Your body is beginning to look like a map, with all those bullet- and knife-scars,' the medic had added. 'Ever think about retiring, Bren?'

'Lately, yeah, I have.'

'Really?' The doctor sounded surprised: he had been merely talking to make conversation while he was examining Madigan's latest wound. 'Well, I suppose you're getting on now . . .'

'Don't make me feel worse than I am, Doc.'

The medic smiled thinly. 'You'll have to do some desk work for quite a spell. This wound will need to drain for at least three weeks.'

'Christ, Doc! Desk work'll kill me.'

'You'll do it, though. You may gripe and cuss but you have enough sense, Bren, to know I don't give such orders lightly.'

That was true enough and while he had hated every minute of it behind the battered desk, Madigan had complied. The assignment to go after Streak and Rango had come just in time to save his sanity. So he was looking forward to checking in at the marshal's office in the morning before stage time.

With a little luck, there might be another assignment that would keep him in the field.

He opened the door of his room and stepped into the low light from the lamp he had left burning, turned way down. Suddenly the light brightened; he dropped the whiskey bottle and swept up his sixgun, crouching as he cocked the hammer, glimpsing a figure sitting in a chair at the table where the lamp burned – brightly now.

'Oh, my God'. Don't shoot!'

Madigan caught the falling hammer under his thumb in time, frowned at the woman sitting pale-faced in the chair, staring at him with wide brown eyes.

She was slim, wore denim trousers and a sand-coloured blouse, a narrow-brimmed hat pushed to the back of her head, revealing straight light-brown hair. She looked to be in her early twenties, had a long brown envelope in her lap.

Madigan stood slowly, seeing that the whiskey bottle hadn't broken – but his long cigarillo had gotten busted and was unsmokable.

'You damn little fool,' he growled, holstering his gun but keeping a hand on the butt. 'I almost blew your head off.' He turned and opened the door. 'Try someone else. I'm not interested in a woman's company tonight.'

She flushed and her eyes narrowed, flashing with anger.

'Who d'you think you're talking to! I'm no whore doing the rounds, looking for a client! I was sent here.'

He frowned, and, not wanting to have an open door at his back, closed it and turned the key in the lock. She looked at him sharply.

'What're you doing?'

'Just a precaution. Who sent you?'

'Ray McInnes.'

23

Madigan knew McInnes. They were old friends from way back. McInnes was the local marshal at Badger's Run up the trail, he had last heard. 'Who are you?'

'I'm Emma McInnes – Ray's daughter.'

Madigan groaned inwardly: nothing like seeing a child you remembered in pigtails with a nest of freckles across the nose and big front teeth, grown up into a fine-looking young woman, to make a man feel his age.

'I guess you must've finished schooling in Denver some time back.'

She smiled a little. 'A few years ago. Dad said he hadn't seen you in a long time. Which was one of the reasons he sent me across here to intercept you. He wants to make sure you call in and see him before you get on the stage.'

'I planned to, although I didn't know he was stationed here. *One* of the reasons, you said. . . ?'

Her smile took on a crooked aspect. 'He said you were kind of – devoted to your job.' She waved the long envelope. 'Message from Chief Marshal Parminter. Dad thought you should have it as early as possible.'

He took it, looking at her openly, smiling a little when he saw that his attention made her uncomfortable.

'You sure have growed.'

'Well, you look considerably older, too!' she returned a little tartly and he laughed.

'Emma, you don't know how true that is! If I feel as old as I look, I'm in trouble, eh?'

She laughed, too. 'Well – you don't look *that* old. I'm sorry I gave you such a start. It was a stupid thing to do, waiting in the dark for a man like you.'

He arched his eyebrows. 'No harm done. You looked at what's in here?'

'I know what's in there,' she temporized. 'In fact, Dad briefed me on it. I have something to add to the message.'

Madigan opened the envelope, read quickly, pursing his lips as he glanced up.

'Captain Kerry's Wild West Show again – Bud Fleischner in Monroe was almost raving about it. He said it was playing at Grand Junction but I see by the timetable here that they'll be ready to move on – when? What's today's date?'

'Twentieth. Yes, they should've started this morning. They open next week in Castle Peak. You'll have plenty of time to get there.'

Madigan folded the papers, looking at her steadily. 'Ray's note says you'll give me more details. . . .'

She nodded, still smiling. 'You're wondering why I'm entrusted with marshals' information. . . .' Her smile slowly faded. 'You obviously haven't heard, but Dad is pretty much confined to a wheelchair now. He was shot in the hip when he walked into a dark church, of all places, one night, supposedly to meet an informant. . . .'

'I heard about the shooting quite a while after it happened. I was down in Mexico at the time. They said he'd recovered. . . .' Leastways, so Parminter had told him.

'Yes – from the wound, but his hip's a real mess.

He can ride, but it's painful. Luckily, he has a young deputy who can handle most of that kind of work.'

Madigan nodded silently: that would have been Parminter's doing, showing a soft side and making sure few people saw it. Ray McInnes had twenty-plus years' service with the marshals, with a fine record, and Parminter must have pulled a lot of strings to keep him on the payroll with a wound that confined him so much. He had gotten around the problem by assigning an active young deputy to McInnes, keeping the older man on full pay.

He must remember to buy Miles Parminter a drink when he eventually returned to Washington.

'What's the worry over this Wild West Show?' he asked the girl abruptly. 'Everyone in Monroe thought it was well worth their money.'

'Yes. But it seems that they're earning a lot more money than they take at their ticket-office. By robbing banks and express offices.'

She gestured to the whiskey bottle at Madigan's feet. 'Why don't you pour us a drink and I'll tell you all about it.'

CHAPTER 3

THE MEXICAN

The group of yelling Indians came sweeping around in a tight curve that lifted dust in a spurting line. They charged out of the haze, shooting rifles and bows, the arrows thudding against the side of the fleeing stagecoach and falling harmlessly to the ground. The shotgun guard was working lever and trigger from a kneeling position as the driver handled the eight-in-hand reins, whipping the rumps of the straining horses in the harness.

One Indian reared upright and tumbled over the back of his racing pony, hitting the dust hard, bouncing aside from the thudding hoofs of his companions' mounts. Another dropped his bow and clawed at his chest, falling sideways, somersaulting away from the main group.

The din was awful, the rumbling of the spinning stagecoach wheels, the gunfire, the war cries, the screams of the two lady passengers in the coach, the snorting of the horses, creaking of the harness and frame of the rocking vehicle. A turn was necessary and the driver was standing now, fighting the reins. The Indians dropped back to allow him to make the turn, then closed again with more din than ever. The fighting guard suddenly threw his rifle in the air and fell over the side of the stage. Pursuing warriors wheeled their mounts around his tumbling body, one hauling rein, allowing a male passenger to lean out of the window and pick him off with his sixgun.

Then the passenger slumped, half-in, half-out of the stage, gun falling. Suddenly the driver reared up and seemed to jump from his seat, landing feet first, tumbling awkwardly. Somewhere a booming voice shouted: '*Runaway stage!*'

There was a bugle call and about ten riders, white men, charged into the arena, making more dust so that the audience in the big burlap walled field had trouble seeing what was actually going on. The rescuers swept in, a man in fringed buckskin standing tall in the stirrups, glittering rifle at his shoulder, firing shot after shot until the magazine was empty. His companions were shooting hard and Indians tumbled to the dust, only a few survivors hauling rein, racing their mounts, followed by those with empty saddles, straight for the big double gateway that was covered with large canvas paintings of Western canyons and distant snow-capped mountains.

The man in buckskin broke from the rescuing group, rode alongside the horses pulling the rocking stage, made a dangerous but agile leap on to an offside-harness lead horse, his own mount veering away as he sawed at the bit, long legs straight, deep voice yelling: 'Whoa, you jugheads! Whoa!'

The audience was on its feet, cheering and waving, shouting as the stage shuddered to a halt and the man in fringed buckskin leapt off, bowed to all points of the arena, sweeping off his wide-brimmed hat, long black hair glinting a little in the sunlight. The grateful passengers alighted one by one.

In the raised announcers' box, a derby-hatted man lifted a speaking-trumpet to his lips and bellowed; 'And so once again the stage to Tucson is saved by the brave and resourceful *Captain – Kerry – Bodiiiiineee!* Let's hear it for our Hero of The Wild West!'

The audience went crazy, climbing over the low calico-and-sapling fence into the arena, running out to greet their heroes who were dismounted now, waiting, the 'dead' men, Indians and white, miraculously resurrected, grinning and shaking hands or accepting slaps on the back, dust rising from their clothing.

Madigan rolled a cigarette, standing to one side: he had stayed in his seat at first but soon realized that would only draw attention to himself, so moved with the flow down to the fence, but stayed on the audience side.

He could savvy the excitement of the folk who had come to see the Wild West Show, for it was one of the best he had seen. He had entered just a little late, in time to see the end of a lady sharpshooter's act, popping strung feathers from a circular cane hoop with a small-calibre rifle, not missing a single one. She was billed as 'Lady Anne Little – Sharpshooter *Extraordinaire* from the Green Woods of Olde England!'

She sure cut a fine figure in her white-fringed buckskin vest and skirt, hat with a jewelled band, gloves coming half-way up her arms, the wind of her passage on the racing white horse as she stood up on the saddle and popped those feathers, moulding her outfit to the shape of her lithe body. He wished he had seen all of her act.

But the rest of the show had been well worth the money: the Indian powwow dances with the colourful costumes, the knife-thrower (a Mexican he thought he knew, billed as *Pancho – Deadly Blade From South of the Border*), some rough-riding and trick-riding by a trio of really fine horsemen, although he thought one man might have been slightly injured, just the way he rode, even though he never missed a cue or a move in the death-defying acts. They were down on the programme as *Trio Courageous*. He had no problem with that for they had to be pretty damn brave to attempt some of the trick-riding they performed.

There was comedy, of course, clown-riders on miniature ponies, running through the rows of children with smoking trousers and pursued by other clowns with pails of 'water' – which, of course, turned out to be cut-up paper when they tossed them so they would 'splash' over the excited kids.

Yeah – you got your money's worth at this show, Madigan decided as he lit his cigarette. It was professional and must cost a hell of a lot to keep on the road and to set up just outside these medium-sized Western towns, only performing twice – occasionally three times if they put on a special matinée, so he had been told.

It would likely cost a lot more money than they made from the admission tickets, although from past experience he knew the Indians (the few real ones, not those whitemen dressed up for the stagecoach attack) would have been hired for little more than food and keep.

Maybe that was why they robbed banks and express offices . . . if they did. For, getting right down to it, it was only a theory, even if it was one put forth by Miles Parminter himself.

Emma McInnes had taken him to see her father, Ray, in the living-quarters above the law offices in Montrose. At the rear, they had had built a zigzag ramp for Ray's wheelchair, but when the girl brought Madigan in the marshal was sitting on a sofa. He made an attempt to get to his feet, with the aid of a stick.

'Stay put, Ray.' Madigan crossed quickly, thrusting out his right hand and so forcing the other to sit back and release his hold on the walking-stick. They gripped firmly and Madigan kept his face blank as he looked down at his friend who seemed to have aged much more than his years. 'How about that little pigtailed Miss Mischief, eh? Where'd she go?'

That brought a smile to McInnes's creased face and his eyes softened as he looked at his daughter.

'She's a beauty, ain't she?'

'Flattery will get you nowhere – either of you,' Emma said. 'Now sit and talk while I make some coffee.'

They had a lot to talk about. The coffee had been drunk and what remained in the pot was cold and they still hadn't spoken of the Wild West Show and Parminter's theory.

Emma brought them around to it abruptly. 'It's way past your bedtime, Dad – I'll give you one hour more and then' – she looked steadily at Madigan – 'then I'll throw you out. Literally, if I have to.'

Madigan arched his eyebrows, winked at Ray McInnes.

'Believe she would.'

'She would,' McInnes told him.

'One hour, gentlemen,' Emma said and left the room.

Madigan shook his head, smiling. 'Plenty of sass.'

'Bosses the hell outta me – and I pass it along to my deputy, of course, but – well, this damn Wild West Show – Parminter's been gettin' complaints for a long time about big bank robberies and express office safes bein' blown right across the country. Seems there's usually three, four men, sometimes only two appear, but a posse will likely find hoofprints of at least three horses.'

'Sound like pros, blasting safes.'

'Know what they're doin'. But they don't always use dynamite or nitro. Sometimes they take the family of the local banker hostage, make him open up – like they did in Estralita, New Mexico. Hit when there was accumulated payrolls for the army at Fort Deacon and that big copper-mine company, Ralls. Then killed the whole blamed family.'

'Heard about that. But where does this Wild West Show come into it? It was playing at Santa Fe when the Estralita thing happened. They'd left there a

32

couple of weeks earlier.'

McInnes nodded. 'Parminter – you know what he's like, 'specially if there's some gang gettin' away with their robberies and tyin' the local posses in knots. . . .'

Madigan knew very well how tenacious and uncompromising the chief marshal could be at such times.

'Well, he started checkin' out everything that could be linked to the places where the robberies took place and he found that every one happened in a town that had been played by Bodine's Wild West Show. Parminter found out that Bodine used the local banks wherever the show was, drawin' money and depositin', transferrin' funds on ahead to the next town and so on.'

'Giving them a chance to find out what was going on with the bank.'

'Sure. Banker was bound to take the "Captain" out for dinner or somethin', get talkin' in general over a few drinks, Bodine askin' how the bank was doin' and what services they provided and so on. Banker'd be flattered to have a man like him interested and he'd be bound to shoot off his mouth. Or a little sly questionin' on Bodine's part would get him whatever info he wanted.'

Madigan frowned. 'Is this the same Bodine got kicked outta the army at Fort Whipple?'

'One and the same. "Sergeant" Bodine then. Quartermaster, makin' some *dinero* on the side by sellin' off army stores, doin' deals with Indian agents and so on. Couldn't prove it enough to make it stick but guess the army decided not to take any chances and booted him out.'

'Read about it. Never met the man.'

'Which is one reason Parminter wants you to go under cover and move in on 'em, find out what's goin' on.'

'Let's see if I've got this. The chief figures they play a prosperous town, Bodine or someone he sends butters up the local banker or Wells Fargo agent and finds out if there are any big shipments of money due – and when. The show moves along to the next venue, but while they're setting up – which would take several days or a week, I'd figure – someone rides back to the place where the money shipment has arrived and steals it. It'd take hard riding but could be done.'

'That's the bare bones of it. If the chief's right, of course.'

'Yeah. Well, it's not bad. They're dozens of miles away when the robbery takes place. They've left a helluva good impression behind because everyone enjoys the show. Bodine's dealings have been all above board – and maybe he has even left a little of his own money behind so it'll be taken along with the rest, make it look good, he's a victim, too. Could work that way, Ray.'

'Yeah, I reckon so, too, but I don't think Bodine would be that smart to figure it out by himself.'

'Maybe not. He could have backing, silent partner or something. . . .'

McInnes poured one final drink for them both, lifted his glass.

'Well, *amigo*, it's your problem – and I sure as hell wish I was comin' with you. Wish I was *able* to come with you.'

They touched glasses and drank.

Now, while the townsfolk were still mobbing the Wild West players in the dusty arena, the afternoon sun filling the enclosure with misty golden light, Madigan wandered over to one of the alleyways between the seats and made his way down to the actual work area.

Quite a lot of folk were already there and he had no trouble blending in, gawking with the others, looking at the horses being tended, seeing the set-up – corrals, chutes, blacksmith's forge, nubbing post (which told him they did some breaking in even 'on the road' as they said in show business), horses of various kinds, including a couple of wild-eyed outlaw broncs he wouldn't have minded a chance to break to the saddle. He saw some of the genuine Indians and the whitemen made up, glimpsed the Lady Anne still in her white buckskin outfit, a little soiled now after her act, and heard her complaining to the announcer in the derby hat as he tried to lead her back towards the arena.

'Dammit, Hush, I'm *tired*! My eyes ache. I caught one finger in the trigger guard and I need to soak it in hot water . . .'

'The public are waitin', Annie,' the derby hat said, unperturbed, almost dragging her now. 'They want to touch you, talk to you. Draw one of your little sixguns and shoot a goddamn crow out of the air or somethin', but Cap says you gotta make yourself available. And if you've a notion to tell him different, then you do it – but *after you go out into that arena and shake a few hands and kiss a few kids*!'

'Goddamn you to hell, Hush Willett!'

Madigan smiled thinly, wondering if that was how an English noblewoman usually spoke to the help.

But she followed Willett out into the waiting crowd.

Madigan saw all he wanted to see, including Pancho, the Mexican, otherwise known as the *Deadly Blade from South of the Border*.

He was also known by another name – 'Cuchillo', which simply meant 'knife' And the man had slipped a blade between the ribs of several men whom Madigan knew of down in Mexico – men and women. They said he was a little loco, used drugs, smoked the cannabis weed. Whatever, the man was a killer and he was on the marshal's list as 'wanted'.

Which gave Madigan all the motivation he needed.

He found the Mexican in the bar of a whorehouse foyer on Little Stem Street later that night after searching through the saloons.

Pancho was drunk – well, maybe not *drunk*, but he was sure excited, high, on something. He was smoking a hand-rolled cigarette and the haze about his head had a funny, pungent smell that Madigan recognized. The man was smoking his weed and enjoying it; enjoying the attention of the three women toying with his clothing, too.

'C'mon, Pancho,' wheedled one with bright, carrot-coloured hair. 'Let's go upstairs again.'

'Ai yi-yi-yi. You like Pancho, eh? Two time already, and you want Pancho again.' He grinned stupidly, waving his cigarette around, pausing with it in front of his eyes to stare at it. 'Ah, my fren', you give Pancho de streng' of *toro!*'

'Hey! How about givin' someone else a turn!' demanded one of the other whores, one with stringy blonde hair. She pushed the redhead roughly. 'Let someone else earn a buck!'

The redhead pushed her back, taller, eyes blazing. 'The man knows he gets his money's worth from me, dearie!'

The blonde swung a hand against the painted face and then the scuffle was on, the hair-pulling and biting and screaming, and the drinkers all gathered around, urging them along, placing a few bets. Meanwhile, the Mexican staggered up the stairs on the arm of the third whore, a younger woman, tugging him as he held back to see how the fight was going.

He paused, angrily shaking off her hand on his arm, staring directly at Madigan who was watching the brawl from the sidelines. The man recognized him, Madigan was sure, but he merely adjusted his hat and moved into the crowd of onlookers. When he looked up, the young whore was standing on the stairs alone, hands on hips, screaming abuse.

Madigan pushed and shoved his way through the crowd, slammed out through the front door and ran down the side alley, reaching for his sixgun.

There was a shadow just climbing to its feet beneath an open window where another half-clad whore was shouting something. The shadow half-turned, saw Madigan, and metal glittered and the marshal stumbled as the knife quivered in the wall beside him.

He held his fire and sprinted after Pancho who

had disappeared into the darkness of the back lanes. There were fences to climb or kick his way through, trash piles to negotiate, rain-worn holes and trenches that tripped him and spilled him to the ground several times.

Pancho must be flying high on his drug-weed; fear, maybe, helping to drive him on into the night. He had run up against Madigan only once before, in a border town called Sabinas, but the man had obviously remembered him instantly. Madigan had wounded him at that time and Pancho had left one of his knives protruding from the lawman's upper gun arm, giving the Mexican a chance to escape. . . .

This time he wasn't going to make it. Madigan couldn't afford for him to get away.

But it seemed that Pancho had managed to do just that. Madigan searched old stables and tool-sheds, even an occupied lean-to behind one of the saloons. He went down as far as the creek, moved cautiously along the banks. No sign of the Mexican.

Madigan had made it his business to get the layout of the town set in his mind earlier, even before going to the show, and he tried to picture it now as he stood beneath a willow tree, gun in hand.

Then something sliced a loose section of his shirt sleeve and cold steel cut his flesh. He staggered and another knife took his hat off his head and pinned it to the trunk of the willow. He threw himself forward full length, wondering how many knives the damn Mex had left, glimpsed a flash of light to his right, by a dark shape that was likely a bush, and he rolled on to his side, shooting twice.

Pancho grunted, and branches and leaves crackled as he was hurled back by the striking lead. By then, Madigan was up and running forward in a crouch, skirting to his left, knowing this man was as cunning as a snake and ten times as dangerous now he was wounded.

Madigan heard him, either crawling away or thrashing about in pain. He moved past the sound and then turned back, saw the vague outline of the man on his belly, trying to crawl into a hollow. There was a gleam of steel in one outstretched hand and Madigan brought his boot-heel down brutally.

The Mexican gave a strangled scream and turned half on his side. Wetness glistened on his shirt front as Madigan knelt, placed his hot gun muzzle against the sweaty throat.

'End of the trail, *Cuchillo* . . You've had a long, bloody run, but it ends here. Unless . . .'

'Wh-what – ees – onless?' The voice was gasping, weak, but Madigan didn't ease up the pressure of the gun.

'What d'you do for Bodine?'

'I *rina caballo*—'

Madigan pressed harder. 'Apart from horse wrangler. You in on the robberies?'

'How – you know – this?' His breathing was faster now as he writhed, trying to get one hand up to the bleeding wound in his chest.

Then his other hand came up with a derringer and thrust at Madigan's face. The marshal threw himself backwards on the instant, firing instinctively, and the derringer's crack was drowned by the

Colt's, but Madigan felt the sting of a ball catching him just above the left ear.

He fell on his back, twisted around, but knew he didn't have to shoot again.

The Mexican's head was hanging by a shred.

CHAPTER 4

WILD WEST WRANGLER

There was a good-sized crowd hanging around the Wild West arena as it was disassembled, the sections of fencing and huge rolls of burlap stacked in large piles. Mostly kids, running about, picking up souvenirs, occasionally 'helping' in a kid's way – that is, getting in the way but tolerated by the sweating, busy men.

Adults wandered around, too, getting in the way as well, but trying to make out how interested they were.

One of these was Madigan. His hair was scorched above his left ear and he had a headache. The cut in his upper arm had been bandaged roughly; it wasn't deep but it had taken a long time to stop bleeding. He wore a different shirt, anyway, and later would find the time to sew up the slash in the material of the one he had worn last night.

He stood around the corral area mostly, nodding to a couple of the men who were stacking saddles and harness gear into the back of a wagon. He noticed a couple of mules amongst the horses. The wild-eyed outlaws were still stomping about their confinement, snorting, looking for trouble.

'Gonna be fun getting them two to behave once they get outta that corral,' Madigan remarked to one of the sweating men, a lanky young ranny with a hooded left eye. The man glanced at him.

'Had my way, I'd turn 'em loose.'

'They can be broke.'

'Not by me.'

'You the wrangler?'

The ranny straightened, pressing his hands against his lower back. 'Looks like I might be. The one we had was killed last night.'

'Hell! What happened?'

'Drunk. Rolled for his money they say, but I reckon he wouldn't've had much left at that time of night.'

'Was he a Mexican?' The man nodded and Madigan added, 'Saw him throwing knives last night. Looked pretty good.'

'Too damn handy with the knives. Won't be missed around here. Leastways, not by me.' The ranny squinted at Madigan. 'You know horses?'

'Worked with 'em most of my life.'

'Need work?'

Madigan hesitated. 'We-ell – I'm *not* working right now but . . . still got a few bucks.'

The ranny grinned. 'Know how you feel. Well, I

better get on, but if you want a job, go see Tex Tyrell. He's down at the blacksmith's right now.'

Madigan said thanks and strolled away, moving across to where men were folding the big painted backdrop canvases, not in any hurry – might look up this Tyrell if he had time or felt like it. That was the impression he was trying to give, anyway.

Tex Tyrell: he had been listed as one of the stunt-riders and Madigan thought he might have been the one he figured was nursing some sort of injury. Just going by the way he moved.

He made his way slowly towards the operational forge; several people, mostly men, were gathered around, smoking, yarning, idly watching the smith shoeing one of the show horses, a big, sleek black gelding. Tyrell was standing by as the man worked on a hoof with a rasp.

Tex Tyrell was a tall, good-looking young man with pale hair and a ready smile for those in the crowd who asked him questions about his acrobatics during the stunt rides. But Madigan got a close look at those blue eyes and thought they looked kind of dead – well, not *dead* exactly, but not matching the man's friendly manner, either. There was a coldness there that was more than just boredom or indifference.

'Yeah, we have falls,' he was saying in a drawl that might have been Texas, certainly from somewhere south of the Mason–Dixon line. 'I had one a week or so ago – strapped up with bandages under this here shirt. Unless we're laid out flat on our backs in a bed somewhere, though, we go through with the act, no matter how much it hurts.'

That impressed the crowd and a couple started to ask more questions but Tyrell turned to the blacksmith.

'See if you can make the shoes a little heavier in the front, Herc. Need a mite more speed on some of them turns and as a hoss's toes hit the ground first, makes sense to give him a little more purchase, right?'

'Whatever you say, Tex,' answered the smith without looking up. He was big-muscled and thick-necked.

Thick-headed, too, Madigan thought, if the man didn't know that a horse's *heel* actually touched the ground first. He was about to speak up but remained silent. Might be something to keep up his sleeve for a little later. . . .

'Feller doing the wrangling said for me to see Tex Tyrell about a job,' he said instead. His words brought Tyrell's head around and those chill blue eyes raked over Madigan, more than likely noticing the fresh shirt standing out against the rest of the trail-stained clothing.

'Why?'

'What?'

'Why would Carney tell you to ask me for a job?'

' 'Cause I told him I've been working with horses all my life. Name's Brennan. Folk call me Bronco.'

Tyrell ignored the hand Madigan offered, still studying the man's face.

'What happened to the hair over your ear?' *Sharp eyes!*

'Got a bad habit of placing a half-smoked cigarette

or cigarillo behind my ear when I want to use both hands. Sometimes forget to put it out first.'

Tyrell grunted, arms folded now as he rested his hips against a workbench. The smith rasped away at the hoof.

'You know what he's doing?' he asked, nodding towards the smith.

'I do. But does he?'

That brought the blacksmith's head up and he squinted his soot-dusted eyes at Madigan.

'The hell does that mean?'

'Heard Mr Tyrell say he needs more speed out of his horse and asked you to make the hoof heavier in front. That won't do it.'

Tyrell watched closely now as the blacksmith straightened, sweaty biceps bulging, the file held like a weapon as he glared at Madigan.

'Then what will?'

Madigan stepped into the area, shouldered the smith aside and picked up the horse's hoof that had been rasped. He gestured to a raised lump near one edge.

'Needs to be shaved down, little by little so you don't expose any tender part. Shoe'll rock on that, throw the horse off balance. Need to forge each shoe individually, too. Each hoof is different.'

Tyrell glared at the smith who frowned.

'I know that,' the big man growled.

Madigan gestured to the four shoes hanging on the horn of the anvil.

'Looks to me like you made them all the same and are about ready to nail 'em on.'

'So?'

'Like I just said, shoes have to be made to fit each hoof. It's the heel that comes down first, by the way.' Madigan looked at Tyrell when he said that and the man said, without showing any interest:

'That a fact.'

'It is. Some horses' feet spread, usually on the back, where they have more depth down to the soles. Bring down the wall of the hoof, rasp the toe down, but don't hardly touch the heel. That brings 'em up and takes some of the strain off the sinews.'

The blacksmith's grimy face was dark now with anger. He hefted the file like he wanted to stick Madigan with it.

'Listen, if I want a lesson in shoein' a hoss – which I been doin' for twenty years – I won't ask you!'

Madigan shrugged. 'Not trying to put down your work. It's something a vet told me – something they've learned from studying horse anatomy.'

'Well, you know where you can stick that.'

'Hold up, Herc,' Tyrell said, suddenly showing genuine interest. 'This stuff with the hoofs. It makes a horse go faster?'

'Doesn't *make* it go faster,' Madigan told him, 'just lets him set down his hoofs more comfortably and gives him a more stable thrust. You do get an increase in speed and manoeuvrability. Shoes last longer, too.'

Tyrell pursed his lips. 'Herc, let him finish doing that hoof.'

'Like hell! He touches it and I go.'

Those blue eyes of Tyrell's chilled way down.

46

'*Adios*, Herc. Pick up your pay from the captain.'

The blacksmith swore, glared at Madigan and suddenly swung the coarse rasp at his face. Madigan whipped his head aside and the tip of the rasp caught the hat-brim, tearing it off his head. He ducked as Herc swung back-handed, hoping to catch him in the face. Madigan came up inside the man's thick arm, rammed the top of his head under that heavy jaw and had the satisfaction of hearing the big teeth *clack* together. Then he hooked a left under Herc's ear. The man's thick neck absorbed the blow and he let out a roar, ran at Madigan with tree-branch arms spread, looking to grab him in a bear hug.

Madigan had no intention of letting that happen – he'd had ribs broken before and they took a hell of a long time to heal. Painful, too.

He ducked under the arms and the smith's weight and motion carried him forward. Madigan hooked two solid blows into his kidneys and the man staggered, clawed at the wall, came around swinging a pair of long-handled tongs. They lifted Madigan's hair, they went that close to colliding with his skull, and he stepped in, rammed a boot-heel down on the man's instep. Herc staggered, floundering, and Madigan hammered him with a barrage of blows, stepped back, came in from the side, took an elbow under the ribs, which he thought had torn his lungs loose. Gagging, he stumbled back and Herc moved in, fast on his feet for such a big man.

He put Madigan down to one knee with a clubbed fist, swung up the tongs in his other hand, ready to brain the marshal. There wasn't much Madigan could do, dazed and gagging, but Tyrell moved fast, caught the descending arm and twisted the tongs loose from the smith's hand. Herc looked surprised, then drove a big fist into Tyrell's face, knocking him back across the forge.

Madigan pulled the dazed rough-rider away from the glowing coals and he spilled to the ground. Herc snarled and moved in on Madigan who crouched now, gritting his teeth against the pain it caused him, hit the blacksmith low, twice. Herc made a sick, moaning sound and doubled up. Madigan's rising knee flung him back so hard against the iron wall that the whole smithy trembled. When Herc bounced off, he ran into three lightning left jabs, setting him up for the whistling straight right that snapped his head back on his thick neck, his eyes rolling up to show the whites.

He waved his arms wildly, trying to get balance and stay upright, then fell like a shot buffalo, snorting air through his big nose hard enough to raise dust and cinders from the ground beside the anvil. Herc didn't seem interested in getting to his feet after that.

Madigan straightened painfully, rubbing his side, and found Tyrell, bloody-mouthed, standing there, holding out his hat towards him, looking at him quizzically.

One finger was poking through the cut in the felt left by Pancho's knife last night.

'Get cleaned up and finish shoeing that horse – your way,' Tex Tyrell said.

'I've got a job here?'

'You're the new wrangler and blacksmith. After

48

you shoe the horse, come over to the captain's tent.'

He gestured to a tent still standing in the western corner of the partly dismantled arena, then turned away, calling to two men to get Herc's barely conscious form out of the smithy. He walked away, dabbing at his split mouth.

The men who had watched the fight closed in around Madigan, saying that beating couldn't have happened to a nicer feller than the blacksmith, who, incidentally, called himself 'Hercules'. Apparently, because of his size, he had been throwing his weight around town, picking fights with the locals. They were all happy to see him beaten. One man brought Madigan a pail of cold water so he could mop up.

'I'd watch my back, though, if I was you,' the man warned quietly. 'He's a mean bastard. Won't forget this.'

'Captain' Kerry Bodine was a man in his mid-forties, hard-muscled and dark-skinned from many years in the army – before that disastrous stint as quartermaster at Fort Whipple had resulted in a dishonourable discharge.

Well, the Old Sarge, as he was once known, had shaken off that stigma, promoted himself to captain, and got together his successful Wild West Show. OK, it was modelled on other similar shows but his was the *best*, he really believed that.

'Give people their money's worth, that's the secret,' he maintained. 'Don't cut corners. You advertise an act, it goes on no matter what; even if you have to throw in a bunch of amateurs, it still goes on according to programme. That's the bible of this business: the programme.'

So far it had worked well enough and he might have gone on making a reasonable sort of living until one time he realized that bankers regarded him as someone important to their institutions, a man who might not have deposited thousands and thousands of dollars, but who was steady and regular with deposits, transfers and the use of banking facilities. Most of the bankers took him out to dinner at least once during his stay in their town – and after a few whiskeys or brandies or whatever their taste leaned towards, they became loose-tongued, wanting to impress Bodine with their importance. . . .

It was crying out to be exploited. . . .

It took only one meeting with each of his top rough-riders to realize they could easily ride back to the town in question, rob the bank – or pay-train if the money was to arrive that way – then hightail it back to the show's present location, many miles from the site of the crime. . . .

It had worked out well and continued to do so.

And would for a long time yet, he was sure.

'Who is he?' Bodine demanded when Tex Tyrell came to tell him about hiring on the new wrangler-blacksmith. The captain was suspicious – wary, really – and would continue to be until he was sure of anyone he was hiring.

'Calls himself Bronco Brennan,' Tyrell told him. 'Knows his horses, it seems.' Tyrell shrugged. 'Dunno too much about him but he looks pretty rugged, in his forties, I'd reckon. Put Herc down pretty damn quick and took a few good punches before he did it. He's tough. We need someone now that Pancho's gone.'

Bodine scowled. 'Stupid damn Mexican! Trust him to get himself killed just when we have a big job coming up.'

'That damn greaser was always riling somebody, specially in the whorehouses.'

Bodine frowned, tapped long fingers against his table. His face was narrow and lantern-jawed and his jaw seemed to jut aggressively now as he nodded slowly.

'All right. Bring Brennan to me when he's finished shoeing your horse and I'll look him over.'

'Right, Cap.' Tyrell paused at the tent entrance. 'I reckon he'll be an asset. Good horses are the key to pulling off these jobs successfully.'

CHAPTER 5

THE WILD WESTERNERS

The destination was Pueblo.

Captain Kerry's Wild West Show moved out of Castle Peak in a long, long wagon train of gear and performers. Many of the construction hands were hired locally at each stop but there were still plenty of riders and fifteen wagons, all loaded to the canvas awnings. The sapling uprights for the big fence were cut at each stop, although some were carried: those ready to assemble into the large gates, and the chute for holding the bucking broncos, ready-made structures that only needed to be slotted and bolted together.

Madigan trailed the wagons, having two riders to help him with the remuda. The outlaws were giving him a lot of trouble, as he had anticipated, and at the first camp, by Remedy Creek, he set up a rope-and-sapling pen, a nubbing-post, and had the outlaws cut out of the main herd, which had been hobbled on a patch of brown grass.

The members of the show gathered as he set about taming the wild-eyed horses. Both were already hostile, eyes rolling, hoofs rising threateningly as he approached with a rope. He managed to get a loop on the piebald and choked the horse down to its knees, letting it know who was boss. It fell over on to its side, legs kicking, and he let it expend some energy that way.

He had two men hold the rope so the bronc couldn't kick while he put a collar rope on him, let it up, the men maintaining pressure on the rope. Then he 'bagged' the piebald, flicking and rubbing the quivering sweating hide with an old sack, getting him used to being handled and the proximity of men. He even tossed a couple of empty coffee cans under the animal, simulating camp noises.

It took about an hour, then he threw an old pack-saddle on the piebald's back, allowed him to kick and buck some, then settled him down, slipped on a rope hackamore and tied his head back a little to a saddlering – not too tight: about what he would feel from the tug of a rein. Then he let him run around the yard while he put the second horse, a chestnut with a white sock on the left foreleg, through the same routine.

He off-saddled both after dark and while the Wild West people broke camp the next morning, he started both horses on yesterday's routine, telling Tex Tyrell he would catch up at the next night camp.

By that time, both horses were a little more manageable. Their heads had been tied down more tightly, and they had been tethered to separate nubbbingposts, allowed to run free at the end of a long, twenty-foot trace-rein, fighting all the strange restrictions of halters and ropes and saddles until they were tired.

Whip Weaver, one of the rough-riders who also gave bullwhip-cracking demonstrations – all the performers seemed to play at least two roles – came back to watch Madigan's breaking-in process. He scowled.

'I tried that piebald after Pancho reckoned he would take a saddle but he tosses his head all the time, like to break my goddamn nose once. An' that's one time too many.'

'A running-rein'll get him out of that habit.'

This was a long strap of leather, leading to the cinch ring, then run back through the bit, giving the rider a lot of extra purchase on the horse's head. When the horse tossed its head, hoping to catch the luckless rider a mauling blow, the strap was hauled tight and the head was pulled down and around and held that way time and again until the horse, if he had any brains at all, realized that it was going to happen each time he played up. In nearly every case it stopped the habit – quickly.

He used long running-reins on both sides then, allowing the horse to run around, shortening gradually, getting him to come off the bit which had now replaced the rope halter. Then, suddenly, he jumped into the saddle, one of the other men riding alongside, getting the piebald used to company and seeing the working horse responding to commands without any undue consequences.

Just the same, Madigan had most of his innards shaken loose by the gyrations and bucking and sunfishing of the piebald. It slammed into the temporary fence until it gave way, then ran for the creek. When it was belly-deep he pulled its head down and around, submerging its nostrils until it began to panic for want of air. Then he let the head up and there was much snorting and tossing, the horse blowing. When it was breathing normally again, it allowed him to pull it around by the reins, and lunged up the bank. He rode it back to the corral, tying it to the nubbing-post once more.

Weaver had been joined by Tex Tyler and they watched as Madigan put the chestnut through the same treatment. When he had the horse tied to a tree, kicking and shaking itself in frustration, he said, removing his gloves from his aching hands, walking a little awkwardly:

'Another day and they'll do what you want – maybe not right away, but I always like to leave a horse with a little spirit, instead of breaking him all the way down.'

'Where'd you learn how to handle hosses like that?' asked Weaver.

'Grew up on a horse ranch in Wyoming,' Madigan said, lying easily.

'Pancho treated 'em a helluva lot rougher than you – and took longer to break 'em to saddle,' Tyrell added.

Madigan shrugged. 'Old-timer taught me. Seems to work. I've seen others talk 'em around, but that takes a l-oo-ng time. Good results, though.'

Over the next three days he worked with the outlaws, just for a couple of hours at a time, and brought them to a point where they seemed content enough to travel with the main remuda without causing undue trouble.

Could be just waiting to make a break, of course, as the wagon train travelled into lightly timbered hill country, but they were noticeably easier to handle.

'You've done a good job with the horses,' Captain Kerry Bodine told him one day. 'Not with just those outlaws, but Tex and Whip and our third rough-rider, Utah, reckon their mounts are better since you reshoed them.'

The captain wasn't as tall as Madigan, nor as heavy, but his proportions were good and his clothes gave him a sleek, rugged look. They had never met before Madigan had been hired, but the marshal knew plenty about this ex-sergeant who had robbed the army and even run guns and whiskey to Indians and Mexican rebels.

'No sense in busting a bronc into the ground. And good shoes can make a difference.'

'Uh-huh. Hard work, though you look pretty tough. I hear you didn't waste any time in putting Hercules down.'

'Had to or he'd've killed me. Couldn't match his strength.'

Bodine nodded again. 'You ever meet Pancho?'

Madigan continued repairing a stirrup shaking his head. 'Saw him throw his knives, is all. He was damn good.'

Captain Bodine grunted. 'Would've taken a good man to kill him. They tell me the shot that finished him was fired from only a few inches from his neck. Never heard of Pancho letting an enemy get that close before.'

'Luck ran out, I guess. Happens to all of us.'

'Mebbe. Well, glad you're with us, Brennan. You like to get into the show proper, do some trick riding, buck-jumping sometime?'

'Not my style, Captain. Rather stay in the background.'

Bodine looked at him sharply. 'Well, I can understand that, if it's what you want. Might come a time when I have to ask you to step in and do something more than wrangle horses and work the forge, though. Be more money in it, of course.'

Madigan grinned. 'Money always talks for me – loud and clear.'

He figured that was what Bodine wanted to hear and the man smiled, nodded, and sauntered away. He seemed satisfied. But, Madigan thought,

He'd been putting out feelers for something.

There was no mistake, Madigan thought, as he helped erect the big fence that would enclose the arena just outside the town of Pueblo. No, no mistake at all.

Pueblo only had a population of about 500 people, much smaller than Castle Peak or other big places Bodine's Wild West show had played. The captain didn't stand to make any money here – there simply weren't enough people.

Working with Jinx Jinks, one of the permanent roustabouts, as they dug deep holes to drop the sapling uprights into, Madigan said casually:

'How the captain expects to make a dollar here beats me.'

Jinx, a rough, hard-muscled ranny in his late twenties, maybe a little short on brains but a very strong
man physically by the look of him, looked up, wiped
the back of a hairy wrist across damp nostrils, and
squinted at Madigan.

'The cap ain't no fool, Brennan. If he sets up the
show here, you can bet he'll make costs and then
some.'

'Way I heard it we only played towns with big
populations.'

'Aw, no, we've played other small towns – some
smaller'n this dump. Not many, mind, it's mostly the
big places we stop.'

'It's because the captain believes in letting as many
folk as possible see our show, Brennan.'

Madigan looked up to see Utah Reeves, the third
member of the *Trio Courageous* rough-riding act,
standing there. Fairly tall, just a little shorter than
Madigan and Weaver and Tyrell, Reeves looked fit
and wore a fair moustache along his upper lip,
making him look a few years older than his twenties –
like Whip Weaver and Tex Tyrell. He wasn't smiling.

'Anyway, what's it got to do with you?'

Madigan leaned on his pick-handle, wiped sweat
from his forehead.

'Like to make sure my pay'll be coming through
regular.'

'You'll get your pay. But not if you stand around
when there's work to be done.'

Utah gave him a hard glare and sauntered off. Jinx
spat after him.

'Don't see him swingin' no pick.'

Madigan agreed. Come to think of it, he hadn't seen the other two doing any hard work, either.

It was set up like an army encampment, tents pitched and spread out like those of a patrol settling in, some tents bigger than others, depending on how many were living in them. Madigan made sure he got a single one – he preferred to be alone, told Bodine that he would be getting up at any hour of the night to check on his remuda. It went down well. Here was a conscientious wrangler at last, not an off-hand lazy one like Pancho.

So, to make it authentic, Madigan did go out and check the remuda a couple of times that first night the tents were pitched. The camp was quiet, fires burned down to glowing embers of ash drifting in the breeze that whistled mournfully through old adobe ruins over on the ridge. The town was a half-mile distant but only a couple of lights glowed.

He swore when he found the ropes of the corral area hadn't been tied properly – leastways, he assumed that had been the problem, as he found them lying on the ground like a couple of long thin snakes. This made for a gap in the fence and most of the horses had strayed.

He woke his two assitants, Cliff and Bobcat, dragged them sleepily out of their bedrolls, and they set off on foot to bring back the remuda. The horses were cropping grass quite happily, didn't want to be moved at first, and surprisingly it was the piebald that eventually took the lead and led them towards the camp. Surprising, because the horse was still giving some trouble: baulking, bucking, fighting reins and saddle. It had thrown Jinx, busted his arm. . . .

This time Madigan checked the ropes himself with Bobcat and Cliff.

'Thanks, boys. I'll bring you breakfast in bed later on.'

They snorted good naturedly and slouched away to their tent, skylarking, a couple of young saddle-bred trail hands earning pocket money before their next cattle drive.

Madigan was tired from working with the horses; he could do with another hand but stubbornly refused to ask for one – fact was, he didn't want Bodine or the other younger rannies thinking his age was catching up with him: age and all the punishment he had taken over the years as a fighting marshal.

He was just a little worried, because this kind of thing had never bothered him before, Maybe he was . . .

Someone was in his tent!

There was only starlight to see by, the quarter-moon, having risen early, was now well on the wane, but he swore the tent wall bulged briefly like someone inside brushing it as they moved about.

By God! he was getting old. He hadn't even strapped on his gun when he'd gone to check the horses!

Well, he still had his fists, and he went in fast through the front flap, knowing he had left the rear flaps tied up. He was right – someone was in there, and he glimpsed the crouching figure going through his saddlebags, turning swiftly as the flap rasped with his violent entry.

The intruder started to get to his feet but Madigan

was too fast, launching himself from the doorway, arms reaching. He knocked the man down and there was a soft grunt, then boots rammed against the side of his head, slewing him sideways. He grabbed anyway, felt cloth, gripped hard, twisted so as to hold on. It tore and an elbow took him on the temple, a knee cracked up under his jaw, and he went down.

Dazed, lights arcing behind his eyes, he made a wild lunge as the man made for the door. He caught a boot, grabbed with both hands and brought the man down. Knees lifted but he wrenched aside, threw himself forward, weight pinning the man now.

Hands clawed at his eyes but he knocked them aside with his right forearm and slugged down with his left fist.

The man bucked once beneath him and went limp. Madigan was surprised – hell, it hadn't been much of a blow. He hadn't expected the thief to crumple that easily.

Panting and sweating, he fumbled for the lantern, groping around for a couple of minutes before he found it, then he snapped a vesta alight and applied the flame to the wick.

The black smoke made him cough as he swiftly adjusted the wick and lowered the glass chimney. The smell of hot kerosene was thick in the tent as he held up the lamp so that it didn't throw a shadow across the thief, who was slowly coming round now, stirring, trying to sit up.

'Hell almighty!' Madigan breathed.

It was Lady Anne Little.

CHAPTER 6

LADY ANNE

'Now that's not very ladylike, ma'am,' Madigan said with a smile in his voice as the woman cursed and and pulled together the ends of the rent in her shirt.

'That shirt cost four dollars in San Francisco, damn you!'

'Fine-looking shirt,' he agreed, seeing now that it was silk shot through with various underlying colours that changed with her movements in the lantern light. 'Looks good on you but you oughtn't to wear such fancy clothes when you come into a man's tent to steal his things.'

'I – wasn't,' she denied, and now he heard the 'lady' tone to her voice as she collected her wits. 'If you must know, I stumbled into the wrong tent in the dark. I was groping about trying to find a light when you set upon me.'

'Oh, is that what I did? I thought I was tackling a

thief going through my saddle-bags.'

He gestured to the open bags, some clothing and a few letters and other belongings strewn about. He also noticed the folded papers she had tucked in behind her trousers belt. She was a fine-looking woman, early thirties, he figured, a 'mature' face was the way he thought of it, smooth bone-structure, fine brows, somewhat slanting green eyes and a wide mouth made for a man to kiss – not that he had any such intention right now. Her figure was shown off by the shirt and cord trousers, better than in her buck-skin shooting outfit, and she was fairly tall, about five-seven.

But there was a coolness, a remoteness about her and he somehow had the impression that this was a cultivated trait, not an entirely natural one. He hadn't had much to do with her but she had usually given him a nod and at least the beginning of a smile if he passed her during the course of his work. He had noticed that that was how she reacted to most of the crew – not enough to call it an acknowledge-ment, and sure not enough for a greeting, but at least it was something.

She started to stir now but froze, suddenly wary, as he moved closer, standing over her.

'I apologize for my mistake, Mr Brennan. Now if you'll allow me to get up . . .'

He offered her his hand. She took it and he helped her to her feet. She brushed herself down, stooping a little as her dark hair touched the sloping roof of the tent.

'You're a blonde when you do your shooting act,'

63

he observed. 'A wig, I guess.'

She flashed a smile but it didn't seem to mean anything, something she had done a hundred times, he figured, before saying:

'Captain Bodine thinks it looks better – flowing golden locks and buckskin. Good-night.'

He didn't move, blocking her exit. The green eyes pinched down and turned cold.

'Would you mind moving – please?'

'Still putting on the lady act, eh? It's kinda late after the way you cussed when you found your shirt was torn.'

She lowered her eyes and he thought she was probably trying to blush but couldn't quite pull it off.

'I apologize for that. I – can hardly help but hear some of the men – including you, Mr Brennan! – the way you carry on when something upsets you during your work.'

'Uh-huh. Sounded pretty authentic to me. Lost your Limey accent and all.'

'Will you – *please* – get out of my way!'

He pushed her back and he saw her stiffen in a defensive position. He reached out and snatched the papers from her belt and she clapped a hand there just too late.

'Found something to interest you, did you?' He chopped off the words now and he saw maybe a flash of fear in her eyes as she watched him unfold the papers. When he looked up his face was tight. 'What were you gonna do with these? Light a fire? Or show them to the captain? Maybe use them against me?'

She scoffed. 'You do have a high opinion of yourself! For an ex-jailbird!'

He said nothing, looking at her coldly, putting the papers back into his shirt pocket.

'You were only released from Yuma penitentiary a couple of months ago, according to those papers. I wonder if Captain Bodine knows that?'

'Question never arose when he hired me.'

Her smile was triumphant now. 'I thought not! You could well be out of a job if I were to acquaint him with the contents of those papers.'

'Maybe. Then again he could be mighty interested to know why you were looking through my things in the first place.'

The smile didn't dim at all.

'Who d'you think requested that I do it. . . ?' She laughed briefly, without humour, pushing past him now as he stood there unmoving. 'Too bad you found your horses so quickly.'

Which only told him that those rope knots hadn't come undone by themselves: she had arranged for someone to lower the ropes and let the horses out, so his tent would be unoccupied while she looked through his belongings.

She ducked through the flaps and then he stepped after her swiftly.

'You gonna tell him now?'

She paused, her face only a blur outside here after coming from the light inside the tent. Calculating. Considering. 'I usually complete any job I am given. But perhaps I won't, now that my own curiosity has been satisfied. I'll decide later.'

She disappeared into the darkness and he went

back into the tent smiling thinly. *That was what he wanted to know.*

She was the one who had been curious. He had a hunch that she would keep the knowledge of the forged prison release papers (arranged by Parminter and forwarded to Roy McInnes) to herself.

Aiming to make use of them in some way.

Yeah – she was some 'lady', this Anne Little. Some 'lady'. . . .

Around noon, Madigan realized he hadn't seen Tyler, Weaver or Utah Reeves today.

'Where's our courageous trio?' he asked Bobcat when taking a drink from the water barrel tied to a shady tree.

'They went somewheres – while you were settin' up your forge.' Bobcat was only about twenty, maybe even a little younger, tousle-haired, freckled and a mite gawky, but a good worker. He spoke with a Tennesee drawl. 'Me an' Cliff cut out some mounts for 'em. They took the piebald, too.'

Madigan paused with the dipper almost touching his lips.

'That bronc is still trouble. Where were they going?'

'Not sure. Said they had some new parts for their act they wanted to try out. Seen 'em ridin' towards them adobe ruins. Might be up there.'

Madigan said nothing, drank his water, rolled a cigarette and then walked over to the corrals. The arena was taking shape now, the men stringing the yards and yards of burlap to the high poles. The gates

would go up later and then there were the seats –
planks resting on angled sapling stands – to be
erected. There was still plenty to do and everyone
had several jobs to get through. The excitement was
rising in the town and folk were riding in from way
out, eager to see the show.

Madigan had some shoeing to do, more shoes to
make to keep on hand for emergencies, and the feet
of the horses to be used in the show had to be
checked for cracks and slivers and stones. Cliff had
started on that and Madigan had intended to lend a
hand but now he walked into the corrals, took down
a rope from the top of a post and tossed a loop over
a young sorrel.

'You goin' someplace, Bronco?' Cliff asked as
Madigan took down a saddle and threw it on the
sorrel's back.

Cliff was almost Bobcat's twin in looks, although he
had a set of buck teeth and was taller. But they had
been cut from the same mould – rangy, stringy-
muscled, would never put on weight, and as at home
in the saddle as a baby in its cradle. Men of the West,
living hard for poor pay, playing hard and spending it
easily, then returning to do it all over again.

'I hear the trio took the piebald.'

'Yeah. Gonna give him a run. Want to take him
into their act, Tex said.'

'Too damn soon. The gunfire'll scare hell out of
him and he'll break. If he runs into the crowd—'

'Moses! Reckon Tex never thought on that!'

'Gonna see if I can catch up with 'em.' Madigan
gave the cinch strap one final yank and went back to

his tent.

When he came back and settled into the saddle, he was wearing his sixgun. He slid his rifle into the scabbard.

Cliff said quietly: 'They crossed the ridge near the ruins.'

Madigan lifted a hand and rode away from the bustling camp. He saw Captain Bodine standing outside his tent with a handful of papers, puffing on his pipe as he read.He didn't look up but somehow Madigan knew he had seen him. Lady Anne was busy practising with her .22-calibre nickel-plated pistols, bringing them to bear on bottle-corks dangling on strings from a tree-branch. The small-calibre guns made whip-cracking sounds and he saw each cork jerk, some torn from their strings.

While reloading,she glanced up, saw him, watched him ride by. He touched his hat-brim but she gave no acknowledgement, merely stared thoughtfully.

He set the sorrel up the ridge to the crest and swung left towards the ruins. Looked like it had been a settler's place, likely building high so as to get a view of the river and right down the valley. To all appearances, it had been razed by fire quite a long time ago.

There was no sign of the *Trio Courageous*.

He sat there, leaning on the saddle horn, looking around, and, way up the valley, in the pale-blue haze, he saw movement that might have been a small group of riders. Then he heard a sound behind him, in the ruins, a clattering of metal against stone, and he didn't wait. Madigan went out of the saddle in a dive, taking the rifle with him, snapping the tie-thongs holding the scabbard. He hit rolling, sliding, and by then two shots had cracked from the ruins, the bullets going wild.

Madigan cleared the scabbard with a wide sweeping swing to one side, levering as he slewed around on his belly, seeing the gunsmoke and the movement of the bushwhacker in a low part of the ruins. He fired and his lead spurted a cloud of adobe dust. The man up there jerked back. Madigan triggered again but the killer got himself safely behind the broken wall.

Madigan squirmed in closer to a log, but it really wasn't thick enough to give him much shelter. The killer saw that, moved to a higher position. Madigan anticipated the man's strategy, had his rifle aimed at the only place the killer could shoot from. As the rifle barrel appeared over the edge, Madigan fired twice. Dust sprayed and a bullet hummed away in a dying ricochet.

But he also saw the dark movement of the man up there rearing back – hit, or just reacting to the shock of the shots he wasn't sure.

That meant a waiting game.

But Madigan wasn't in a waiting mood. He was slightly upslope from part of the ruins here and he rolled silently across the grass to a line of broken, fire-blackened wall and charred timbers. He picked up two long splinters in his thigh as he crawled across, watching the higher part all the time. He couldn't see the killer at first but then the rifle boomed and lead slammed into the ground bare inches from his face. He reared back, instinctively rolling to his left. Another bullet almost took his head off, spurting dust from the brim of his hat.

Then he heard the lever up there working – and working. The man was out of ammunition, had to reload.

Madigan dropped his own rifle, thrust to his feet and began pounding up the slope, sixgun sliding into his hand. The dark shape up there heard him, saw him, and the partly reloaded rifle barrel swung towards him. But the killer was too hasty, worked his lever, shut it too quickly – and jammed a shell half-way into the breech.

Madigan actually found that out later; at the time all he knew was that the killer's gun didn't fire. But Madigan's Colt did, bucking in his fist, two fast shots, at least one hitting home with that unmistakable meat-cleaver sound of lead striking flesh.

The man grunted in pain and seconds later Madigan was standing over him, saw the blood from three different body wounds on the dirty, charcoal-smelling clothing before he recognized the bush-whacker.

Hercules.

The blacksmith was still alive, blazing eyes staring up at his killer, blood trickling from a corner of his mouth. Madigan hunkered down beside him, pushed the man's rifle well out of reach. He rapped him on the bridge of the nose with the hot barrel of his Colt. Hercules winced, jerking his head back.

'Bastard!' he croaked, blood bubbling in the back of his throat.

'Not even trying yet, Herc. You look bad. Might

last the day. Be mighty painful if you do. One of them's a gut wound, another's tore up your lung I'd say, from the way you're breathing and spitting blood. Third's somewhere in your chest. You're a real mess. One bullet, right . . . here . . .' Madigan pressed the Colt's muzzle between the man's eyes, 'and it's all over. No more suffering.'

'Do – it – then!' Herc gasped.

'Well, it's gonna cost you. Tell me who set you up to bushwhack me and answer a couple more questions and I'll do it for you.'

'Go – to – hell!'

Madigan sighed and stood up, lowering the gun hammer and sliding the weapon back into his holster. He pushed his hat back on his head.

'Your decision. I was you, though, I'd take the quick bullet. Had me a pardner once, shot up like you. Took him two days to die. Didn't have a bullet left between us, after a fight with some Comanches down on the Llano, not even a decent knife, and I didn't fancy having to saw and hack at his throat to get to that big artery. Had to listen to him coughing up his lungs, his innards working their way outta the belly-hole, ants chewing on 'em – screaming like you never heard except when an Apache was torturing a cavalry man. Still gives me nightmares and that was – aw, hell, must be nigh on twenty years back now. Finally choked on his own blood.'

'Utah,' Herc grated, blood spilling over his chin as he squirmed around listening to Madigan. 'S-said you'd come after that – that piebald. He left – tracks up – this way.'

'That gospel?' Madigan asked soberly and Hercules nodded several times, coughing now. He looked up with wild eyes full of terror as blood bubbled up into his throat.

'Aw, hell, I got no way of knowing if you're telling the truth or not. *Adios*, Herc. At least you'll be used to the heat down in Hell.'

The bullet drove home and Hercules slumped.

Madigan reloaded, wondering why Utah Reeves would want him dead. Might not necessarily be Reeves, of course. He could just be the spokesman for whoever was really behind the set-up. Thing was, someone didn't want him around, even tried to make it look like Herc had borne a grudge over the fight. Question was: why? He hadn't put a foot wrong yet. No one could know he was working under cover.

If the forged prison release papers had upset Bodine, he only had to fire him to be rid of him.

That's if Lady Anne had even told Bodine about the papers. . . .

Hell, there were so many 'could haves' that his head was spinning.

This wasn't working out to be as straightforward as he had figured. With so many people to watch out for, he was going to end up with a crick in his neck like lockjaw.

Or a bullet in his back. Or his belly. Or . . .

He was a target, that's what he was. And unless they used trickery in the show, the people who wanted him dead were all marksmen.

Might's well have a bull's-eye painted between my shoulder blades, he complained to himself bitterly.

CHAPTER 7

BACKTRAIL

CASTLE PEAK ASSOCIATED BANK OF COLORADO.

That was what the sign said on the window: gold lettering against a dark-green background with the name, Aaron Marcus, President, done in white underneath.

It was quiet enough in town this noon. Quiet, though Main Street was still carrying a good deal of traffic, but not as much as during the hours either side of noon. The boardwalks were emptier at this time, a fact Tex Tyrell had noted when the Wild West Show had been playing the town. He wasn't sure why and it didn't really matter, it was just a fact that suited his plans.

The reason was that Castle Peak was a town of community-minded citizens and 'good neighbours', who had developed a set of habits they found hard to break. They were proud of their town and the founding fathers who had set up a list of ordinances that benefited everyone. These same pioneers had also hired a tough lawman to implement these ordinances, and, though that man was long dead, as the town grew people came to realize it prospered mainly because the law had prevailed. They were mostly 'good' citizens, in other words, and did their part to help make sure the streets stayed safe for their families. They worked hard whether they were farming or raising cattle. This town was actually instrumental in getting Colorado admitted to the Union in 1876 because it was such a shining example of how folks from all walks of life could get along.

There weren't too many places like that in the Wild West.

The rich country in the huge Castle Valley which lay to the north-west of the Peak sure helped: there were fine pastures for cattle, rich river-bottom soil for farms, timber for a lumber mill, and, within easy working distance, a line of limestone hills for making cement. Jobs for everyone who wanted to work – and those who didn't did not last long in Castle Peak.

It was mighty close to Paradise, or so folk who lived there claimed and, mostly, few men disputed this.

So with all that fine land and fat cows and ripe fruit and vegetables, there just had to be a lot of cash money flowing through the Castle Peak branch of the Associated Bank of Colorado.

Captain Bodine had made sure of that when his troupe was in town.

Although it was a fine sunny day, the three men who tethered their mounts in the far end of the alley between the bank and the druggist's wore long oilskin slickers of a dark-brown colour, indistinguishable from thousands of others available in any Western general store. The trio had buff-coloured hats with wide brims, downturned above their eyes, throwing deep shadows on their faces, distorting and confusing features like noses and mouths and eyes.

One man carried a sawn-off shotgun and he checked the loads in the breech before snapping the gun closed and pushing it under the slicker. He reached his right hand through the slit pocket and held the gun out of sight. The other two checked sixguns, tugged their yellow workgloves more tightly on to their hands and moved to the rear corner of the bank building.

Tex Tyrell slipped his watch out of his pocket, fumbled at the folds of the slicker so he could read the face. He showed it to the other two men and they nodded, turned their attention back to the red-painted rear door set in the brickwork behind a heavy iron-barred gate. They eased back into the shadow of the wall when they heard a key turn in the door. It swung open and they saw a man's hands as he fumbled at a bunch of keys on a ring and unlocked the barred gate.

As he stepped out – a middle-aged man in a finely tailored broadcloth suit and wearing a brown derby hat – the three men moved in, even as he began to close the iron gate.

'Just leave it as 'tis, sir,' Whip Weaver said in a conversational tone. 'We're going in to transact some business.'

The man turned, half-smiling, speaking before he

noticed the guns in the hands of these men who were wearing slickers on such a warm sunny day.

'I'm afraid this is a private entrance. I'm the hank president and I use it . . .'

He broke off, jaw hanging as he saw the guns in their hands.

'You use it each noon to come out and cut across the alley to that lane that leads to a footbridge over the crick and on to your property where that fine, fine house sets astride the highest piece of land in town. Yeah, we know all that, Aaron. Now what you gotta do, is just miss your lunch today—'

'Aw, that won't be necessary,' said Utah Reeves showing Aaron Marcus his shotgun. 'Aaron might be a little late, is all, but long as he co-operates his lunch won't be cold when he gets home.'

Tyrell leaned towards the stunned bank president.

'You *are* gonna co-operate, ain't you, Aaron? Reason I ask is because if you don't, one of my pards here is gonna take your private path clear up to your kitchen door and keep your wife and family – and your servants, let's not forget them – company until you do . . . I mean, you might say, their lives are in your hands, right?'

Marcus swallowed. He was nervous, pale, sweating, but he was game, slammed the gate and tried to toss the ring of keys over the fence into the garbage pit behind the druggist's shop. Tyrell caught his hand, twisted the keys from his grip quickly, and gunwhipped him with his Colt's barrel. Aaron Marcus made a strange whimpering sound as he stumbled to one knee.

'Aw, look at that!' said Utah, shaking his head. 'Ain't that a damn shame? He's got mud all over the knees of them nice grey pants.'

'Lucky it ain't blood,' growled Tyrell.

'Now, gents,' said Whip Weaver calmly. 'No need to get excited. Mr Marcus just needed to be shown that we're serious. I mean, just think if that had been your wife who was gunwhipped, sir. Mmmmm, reckon it would hurt her a lot more'n it hurt you. Then there's that young son of yours, and – how could I forget! – why, you've got a blossomin' young filly of a daughter, must be all of twelve or thirteen, right. . . ?'

Blood was trickling down Marcus's face as Utah grabbed one of his arms and hauled him to both feet. He allowed the man to take out a white kerchief and hold it against the cut in his forehead. The derby hat had somehow gotten trampled underfoot.

'All – right – I – I heard about that terrible bank robbery at Estralita – I – I'll co-operate. Just don't harm my family, please!'

'Polite, ain't he?' chuckled Tyrell, hitting the man's shoulder roughly.

'Do what you like to me but – *please* – leave my family alone!'

'Brave little feller, ain't he?' opined Utah Reeves.

'You have nothing to fear, sir,' Whip Weaver assured him. 'Long as you do what you're told. Now, time's getting on and – we're on our lunch hour, too! So let's move it.'

The trio chuckled and Marcus opened the red door and they shoved him stumblingly down the narrow passage leading into the rear of the bank building. . . .

Before they reached the big safe behind the counters in the business section of the bank, which fronted Main, they had gunwhipped two startled clerks, one female, the other a pimply-faced youth who had been trying to work a hand down her bodice.

'Naughty, naughty,' Tyrell admonished as they collapsed in a heap. Then a man entered from the front, saw the guns and captive bank president, dropped the papers he was holding and started to turn back up the passage, shouting,

'Bank robbers! Bank robbers!'

The last word was drowned in the roar of Reeves's shotgun and the man's body, arched like a drawn bow, was blown into the front section of the bank, broken and bloody.

There were screams and panicked cries and some customers lunged for the street doors, but Weaver was too fast for them, reached the etched half-glass doors and shot the bolt across, swiftly pulling down the blinds. He wagged an admonishing finger at the townsfolk and they all cannoned into each other as they tried to stop from colliding with him as he barred their way.

'Watch for the sheriff,' snapped Tyrell, careful not to mention names. He jerked his head at Utah. 'Set 'em filling the bags. . . .'

They almost got away without any more trouble but the pimply-faced clerk came round and he managed to pull a short lever underneath the desk where he worked. This lever released a red flag on a short pole fixed to the front of the bank building which had no awning so it could be readily seen by anyone on the street.

It meant, of course, that a robbery was in progress inside the bank and within a minute of the flag's appearance, Sheriff Barton Early and his deputies were grabbing their weapons from the glass-fronted gun cabinet in the law office.

Barton Early was a bull of a man, his clothing always seeming to be too tight for him. But it was muscle that bulged it, not flab. He was about forty, mean-eyed and hard-faced, balding – but he compensated for this by allowing the fringe to grow down almost to his shoulders. His voice was heavy and coarse.

'Bank's front doors are closed, so means they'll try to run by the side or rear doors.' He spoke rapidly to his three deputies as he handed out weapons. 'Bill, Tate – you two go to the rear and if they's any hosses tethered there, why, you loosen the cinchstraps and find someplace to hide.'

'Be best to run the hosses off, wouldn't it, Bart?' asked the rail-thin man named Tate.

'No, it dang well wouldn't!' snapped Early, impatient at having to explain his orders. 'They see the broncs waitin' and they jump for the stirrups and the saddle and whole shebang comes loose and they end up on the ground. Like takin' candy from a baby then, just walk out with your guns cocked . . .' He spun to the remaining deputy, a young man barely out of his teens. 'Mort, you go watch the side door –

but I don't think they'll use that because it can be seen from Main – and before you settle down to watchin', you grab half a dozen men goin' by and send 'em to me. I aim to deputize 'em in case we need a posse after all. . . .'

The deputies scattered to do their duty and Barton Early loaded his long-barrelled Greener twelve-gauge, selecting brass-based shells filled with double-0 buckshot, designed to blast a hole in flesh, human or animal, big enough to stick your hand through.

When Barton Early went after a law-breaker, the man was given only one chance to surrender. After that it meant dying or being horribly wounded.

Already a small crowd had gathered around the bank's doors and they scattered when Early lumbered up, cussing them out in his gravelly voice.

'Get the hell away from them doors! Clear out of it – or grab a gun and help. Otherwise vamoose, pronto!' He roughly shoved a couple of men aside, banged the shotgun's butt against the wooden panel of the door below the glass. 'You in there! We got the bank surrounded! Now throw down your guns and come out or we're comin' in – and if anyone in the bank is hurt, I promise you, there ain't a one of you gonna see a court room and trial!'

There was utter silence for a long twenty seconds, even the traffic stopping on Main. Then thunder roared and glass and wood of the doors shattered and big Bart Early was blown back across the walk. His ragged and bloody body rolled like a barrel of beer into the gutter.

Screams came from the bank followed by three fast gunshots. Folk on the street scattered and Mort came running out of the alley, wide-eyed, leaving the side door unguarded. Tate and Bill, older and more experienced, although shaken and edgy after the roar of the shotgun, not knowing if it was the sheriff's or the outlaws', stayed put. They hadn't had time to loosen the cinchstraps all the way on the getaway horses and now they took cover, waiting to see developments. . . .

Out front, Mort ran to kneel beside the bloody form of the sheriff, and men he had ordered to go and be deputized ran to get their guns. Not that it would help Barton Early.

More full of vinegar than good sense, Mort snatched up the unfired Greener and ran to the shattered door, using the barrels to smash jagged glass and splintered wood aside, looking in. Inside, folk were running towards the door that now hung on twisted hinges. Mort kicked one door off completely, motioning to the people to come on through. He saw the slicker-clad bandits inside and fought his way past the people thrusting against him, fired the shotgun, but the charge went into the roof and brought down a lot of plaster and splintered ceiling laths.

It also brought Tex Tyrell's attention to Mort and his gun came up blazing. Mort shuddered as lead hammered into his lean body and he went down under the feet of the panicked crowd. It probably saved his life because Tyrell was unable to get a clear shot at him and Weaver was yelling to get the hell out, but:

'Don't leave the cash bags!'

They charged out through the side door, which was totally unguarded now, and made for the rear of the building. Tate and Bill were crouched at the corner of the brick wall, and were only now turning at the sounds of the pounding boots of the outlaws.

Tate yelled; '*Jesus!*' swinging around with his rifle and Reeves let him have the second barrel of his sawn-off shotgun. Some of the buckshot stung Bill who rolled away frantically, rammed the butt of his rifle against his hip and got off a single shot before Tyrell nailed him dead centre with a slug from his smoking Colt.

They ran to the skittish mounts and hit the stirrups in flying leaps. Utah and Tex fell, their saddles sliding half-way around the mounts' bodies. Whip Weaver's mount was the one the deputies hadn't had time to work on and he settled into saddle, draping two bags of cash over the saddle horn, lifting the reins – then stopping in astonishment as he saw his two pards on the ground, cursing and caught up in the folds of their long slickers.

There was yelling coming from the alley down the side of the bank building and Weaver shouted at the others.

'Come on! Move!'

He fought his prancing horse, saw the first of the townsmen with guns coming around the corner. He triggered until his sixgun was empty, then spurred his mount away from there, heading towards the creek and the narrow footbridge that led on to the bank manager's land. He reloaded his gun as he rode and when Aaron Marcus's family and servants appeared on the porch, looking down towards the town where all the gunfire came from, he fired indiscriminately into the group.

Men, women and children all screamed and tumbled about on the porch, survivors frantically trying to fight their way back into the big house. Weaver bared his teeth and rode on, seeing, at last, that Tex and Utah were coming. They had jettisoned their saddles and were riding bareback. *And without their slickers!*

He hoped they hadn't left the damn money-sacks behind, too.

Then he saw the first of a mounted posse forming and he concentrated on getting away, wondering how in hell evervthing had gone so wrong after such careful planning.

CHAPTER 8

CHASES

Madigan tracked the piebald way up into the hills. It was without saddle or bridle when he found the animal grazing on a bunch of sweet grass on the bank of a creek.

Obviously it had been turned loose by the trio. He smiled grimly: likely gave them too much trouble. Or, it had simply served its purpose of leading him near the adobe ruins so Herc could bushwhack him.

The horse's belly looked to be pretty full. It lifted its head, regarded him kind of dreamily and went back to grazing, moving away only a few feet. Of course, in the maddening way animals have, it kept that distance between itself and Madigan each time he approached, without effort or even noticing him, barely missing a mouthful of grass.

Madigan was weary and gritty with sweat and dirt and more than a little angry at himself, because he had put a mark on each of the horseshoes he had forged for the piebald, knowing it was not yet broken and that it would wander at every opportunity, even if hobbled, and he would be able to track it easily. He could – and would – put a stop to the wandering when they were on the trail again, simply by using a shin-tapper hobble made with eighteen inches of chain and a leather cuff. By buckling the cuff to a fetlock, when the horse moved quickly, the chain would lift and start cracking the other unhobbled foreleg. After a dozen or so times any half-smart horse got the message that a little shuffling movement was the only way to avoid this painful beating and so it wouldn't wander far – or fast.

He figured he wasted over an hour trying all the subterfuge he knew to get hold of that piebald, hoping it would show signs that it was learning and willing to give a little. No, not that damn piece of crowbait. So, in resignation, admitting the horse had won this round, he unshucked his rope and shook out a loop.

So the goddamn horse immediately took off at a run and he had to swing into saddle and spur after it! It led him on a chase through brush and timber and finally cornered itself in a dead-end draw. Just as well, or he'd have been riding into the sunset! When he eventually had the piebald roped and hauled alongside it gave him a rolling eye and he swore there was a *grin* on that ugly jughead face!

He was more angry at himself than the horse, though: here he had spent all this time tracking the animal which had obviously been deliberately turned loose by the trio to keep him busy while they – *what?*

He was a damn fool, and he tried to fight down a growing admiration he had for this frisky animal trotting alongside as he rode back down out of the hills.

Now he he was stuck with the piebald, or had to find somewhere to leave it, securely, while he tried to pick up the trail of the others. He had finally figured out why Bodine had chosen such a small place as Pueblo for his road show. *He didn't have a choice!* Not if, as Madigan suspected, the trio were to ride back to Castle Peak and hit the bank there. It was the biggest in this part of the country and there was no large town close enough to give Tyrell, Weaver and Reeves time to ride back to Castle Peak and back again to Pueblo and be ready for the performance. So Bodine *had* to play a small town within reach of his target. His explanation that he wanted to give everyone a chance to experience his Wild West Show went down well enough with folk who would never be able to reach some of the larger towns they played.

There was no bank to check on and earmark for the next robbery in Pueblo. Which might be just as well for Bodine: it was time to give things a rest. There had been a lot of robberies and the Estralita massacre had drawn too much attention from the law. Things must be pretty damn edgy for Bodine and his crew right now. But they couldn't afford to pass up the chance of a big pay-off in Castle Peak.

If Bodine had any sense it would be their last job for quite a while.

But he had let them slip through his fingers – all because of some damn horse he had been unable to break in thoroughly!

86

'Maybe I better take a rest, too,' he murmured half-aloud, scouting for tracks of the trio. He hated to admit it, even to himself, but – he was slowing down, starting to make mistakes. And no marshal could live long doing that.

Look at the way he had almost ridden into that headshot from Hercules back at those adobe ruins. His mouth tightened – well, it would be mighty interesting to see what Utah Reeves had to say about *that*!

If he ever caught up with the son of a bitch. . . .

Stiffly, he climbed down from the saddle once more, examining what he figured was a reasonably fresh half-moon chip out of the edge of a rock. And as he reached for the rock itself with his right hand, he felt the searing burn of rope being ripped across his left palm, fell back from his squatting position and sprawled – watching the snorting, whinnying piebald toss its head as it ran off, trailing the long rope dangling from about its neck.

Madigan gave up, sat up, took out tobacco and papers and rolled a cigarette.

'To hell with it,' he murmured as he fired up.

The trio had only just managed to shake off the posse and make it out of that wild country north-east of Castle Peak alive and mostly in one piece.

Whip Weaver couldn't be sure, but it looked to him like the posse was being led by the young son of a gun whom Tyrell had blasted in the bank but hadn't finished off. The kid was game. He glimpsed him once when they were holed up in some rocks, caught the flash of crude bandage around one upper arm and across his chest. Not only game, looked like he was plenty tough, too.

And he was using his brains. There were six or seven townsmen in the posse, and he split their ranks, some riding slightly to the south so that if the trio separated or made a run in that direction his men could get after them with no waste of time and minimum sacrifice of distance. The other part of the posse could continue in the present direction or swing more to the north if necessary.

'OK!' Weaver gritted. 'But s'pose we stick to this line – then turn and fight, you bastard!'

Tyrell and Utah heard and they snapped their heads up fast, both angry that they had had to ride bareback. The sacks of money were jammed into their laps because of the absence of either saddle horns or bags.

'You're not thinking of making a stand against 'em?' asked Tyrell. 'After the way you shot up that banker's family?'

Weaver pointed grimly. 'Look at that dust cloud way back. Could be another posse formed by the townsmen. So we have to stop these *hombres* and lose ourselves in the hills before the others catch up.'

As Tyrell was about to ask just how in hell he aimed to do that, Weaver reached into a saddle-bag and brought out a bundle of dynamite sticks, a short fuse already hanging from it. He grinned tightly at their startled expressions.

'That narrow pass through the hills,' he said.

'Chino Pass?' asked Utah Reeves. 'Man, that's north! Soon as they see us swing that way they'll cut over the mesa and head us off.'

'Not if we don't make our swing till the last minute,' Weaver told him. 'Ride lickety-split dead ahead as if that's the only way we want to go, then when we reach that clump of three dead trees—'

'The Dead Men.' Tyrell dropped in but Weaver only looked at him bleakly, otherwise ignoring the comment.

'We hit the pass, you two take my horse while I climb the slope, plant the dynamite and light the fuse. I'll run to that flatrock overhang and drop into the saddle again and we get the hell out of there.'

'They might not be into the pass when she blows,' cautioned Tyrell.

'The hell's it matter!' snapped Weaver, impatient now. 'The wall comes down and blocks it with a couple hundred tons of rock. They don't have to be *in* the pass. They still can't get through. They'll have to ride back ten miles to skirt the range and by then we'll be about ready to hit the show ring and strut our stuff.'

There was no alternative, anyway: by now they could see a lot of dark specks under that new cloud of dust, rapidly closing on this position. The townsfolk were out for their blood.

As it happened, the original posse under Mort was only yards from entering the knife-blade narrow pass called Chino when the dynamite blew, high up on the southern wall.

It went with a roar and a crash of shattering rock and flying dirt, flame spiralling up as the wall bulged and bellied before erupting into a deadly storm of jagged shale and basalt, thundering down out of the sky.

Two horses squealed and whinnied as they were struck heavy blows by fist-sized chunks, unseating their riders who had to scrabble and somersault and throw themselves wildly aside to escape the hoofs of the panicked mounts. The posse men fought their reins, cussing, coughing as choking clouds of dirt and dust engulfed them. They had come within seconds of dying under that avalanche. Two more men tumbled from their saddles and staggered after their fleeing mounts. Mort, already wounded and one arm not functioning fully, fell and lay gasping on his side as the posse man still mounted snatched the flying reins of Mort's horse and hauled it to safety.

Numbed and dazed by the explosion, ears ringing, Mort crawled away, gasping. He was beaten, and knew it. They would have no chance of overtaking the lousy thieving murderers now.

Well, he had tried, but the fact was, the outlaws had got away with thousands of dollars and the murder of several citizens.

There would be no sheriff's star waiting for him back in Castle Peak.

Still bitter about failing to pick up the tracks of the *Trio* that afternoon, Madigan had put the protesting piebald through a rough routine after finally bringing the horse back to the corrals.

It had given as good as it got and by sundown, both man and animal were sweating and stiff, muscles throbbing. Madigan told Cliff to rub down the piebald and give him some oats later when he had cooled, maybe mixed with just a little grain. The horse had spirit and Madigan was ready to admit to having a sneaking affection for him.

He went down to the river and stripped and scrubbed grime from his lean, scarred body with sand and lye soap and washed his dirty clothes. He was drying himself on a scrap of towel in the fading afterglow when he saw a movement in shadows under the trees.

He dropped the towel and, buck naked, dived for his sixgun resting on the coiled bullet belts beside his fresh clothes, somersaulting as he came up on one knee, the gun covering the shadows.

'Step out where I can see you!' he said.

There was a pause and then Lady Anne Little came into view, holding a bundle of clothing and a bar of soap.

'My! That was *fast*, Brennan!' she said, undisguised admiration in her voice. She walked closer as he stood, unworried about his nakedness, the gun following her movements, hammer spur still back beneath his thumb. She stopped a couple of feet away, looking him up and down. Her gaze flashed to his face and she said soberly, 'You begin to interest me, Brennan.'

'I'm about to get dressed. Hope that won't spoil things for you.' He sounded annoyed and she smiled.

'Not at all. I'm wondering how you got all those scars. If I'm not mistaken, I see marks left by bullets, arrows, a knife or tomahawk blade. And you are a lot more muscular than you seem when dressed. And the way you dived for that sixgun! I think you are a much more dangerous man than anyone believed, Bronco Brennan.'

He had lowered the hammer now, picked up his trousers and pulled them on, saw her watching curiously as he dressed in the rest of his clothes.

'I'm wondering how a man in his forties could collect so many battle scars, yet still move like a bolt of greased lightning.'

'*I'm* wondering how a "lady" can recognize what made those scars.'

She shrugged. 'Oh, the British Army has been a tradition in our family for generations. I can trace my ancestors back to the time of William the Conqueror. My – brothers were all wounded at one time or another. Some scars collected in battle, some – well, we've always been a family touchy about our honour.'

He ran his fingers through his damp hair, pausing just before jamming his hat on his head.

'Duelling?' When she frowned, he added: 'Fought a duel myself once. Some self-styled gent in New Orleans fancied I'd sullied his name. Pistols at dawn, very formal, even down to the *coup de grâce* by the attending doctor.'

She nodded. 'I suppose I shouldn't be surprised about you, Brennan. Not after finding those prison release papers in your saddle-bags.' Her gaze sharpened as she added: 'I wonder why a man would carry such things around. They're incriminating, aren't they?'

'One way of looking at it – but a lot of these damn

sheriff's don't keep up to date with their Wanted dodgers. They find an old one with my picture on it and they want to throw me in jail. I produce papers that prove I've already served my time and . . .' He shrugged.

'I – see. I've been toying with the idea of expanding my shooting act. I've yet to see you use a gun, of course, but if I can work out a satisfactory addition to my act – would you be interested?'

He pursed his lips, wringing out his washed clothing, hanging it on the low branches of a tree.

'Dunno. I like working with horses. Depends on what you were offering.'

Their eyes met and held. 'Well, I may give it some more thought. Now, if you'll excuse me . . .'

She indicated her bundle of clothes and the soap.

Madigan grinned slyly. 'Could scrub your back for you.'

'And die in the attempt,' she told him soberly, showing him one of her small nickel-plated .22-calibre pistols under the clothing bundle. Cocked and ready to fire.

He grinned 'Yeah. Guess I best go find Bobcat instead. I've got a chore for him.'

'Oh? He rode out a little while back. Whip Weaver came in and asked him to do something for him. He threw a couple of saddles into a buckboard and drove out just before sundown.'

She was watching him closely, saw his frown, seemed to be waiting for his reaction.

His face was blank when he nodded.

'Well, it can wait. Enjoy your bath.'

He made his way back towards the arena, paused and looked back.

'By the way – better pick up your accent. It's been dropping all over the place these last ten minutes.'

By the time Madigan came out of his tent, hair combed and still wet, wearing his boots and gun rig, Bobcat was back from his chore. He stopped the buckboard down behind the corrals. Madigan strolled across as the young roustabout unharnessed the team.

'Been looking for you.'

'Whip asked me to take a couple saddles up to the adobe ruins. Said Tex and Utah were up there. Someone stole their saddles from wherever they'd been all day.'

He seemed edgy and Madigan asked why. Bobcat, mouth stretched tight, reached in over the side of the buckboard tray and threw back a rumpled tarp that was lying along one side.

It revealed the body of Hercules.

'*He* was up there at the adobe ruins, too. Someone shot him, four, five times looks like.'

'What would he be hanging around for after the captain fired him?' Madigan asked, for something to say. By now others were coming across, seeing that something was wrong.

'Dunno. But he was kin to Utah.'

The crowd arrived, all asking questions. Madigan moved away as Bobcat, seeming happy enough at being the centre of attention, told his story – what there was of it. Captain Bodine walked across and

Madigan saw Whip Weaver standing by his tent, rolling a cigarette. He guessed he had already seen Herc's body, up at the ruins.

'Where were you that someone could steal a couple of saddles?' he asked and Weaver looked through a cloud of smoke, his eyes narrowing.

'Nothing to do with you where we were, Brennan. The saddles were stolen and now they've been replaced. Forget it.'

'Touchy fellers, you and your pards.'

'No. Just don't like *hombres* with long noses poking 'em in where they're not wanted.'

'Fair enough,' Madigan said easily, turning at the sound of riders coming in. Utah and Tex Tyrell.

They reined in outside Weaver's tent and as they swung down, Utah Reeves glared at Madigan.

'Take care of the horses, Brennan.'

'Bobcat'll do it when he's finished over at the corrals.'

Utah turned angrily. 'I'm telling *you* to do it. You're the wrangler.'

'Let's forget the horses and who's what for a moment,' Madigan said and all three men tensed, watching him, closely.

'Brennan, I think you sound a mite too big for your britches,' opined Tex Tyrell coldly.

Madigan kept his gaze on Utah. 'Went after that damn piebald you fellers took for some reason. Led me up past the ruins. Someone took a couple of shots at me.'

They composed their faces, unsmiling: it was all news to them. They tried to look interested.

'I guess you shot back,' Weaver said crisply.

Madigan just stared and Utah swore softly.

'You killed Herc!'

'He was doing his best to kill me. Back-shooting bastard.'

'You son of a bitch! He was kin of mine!'

'Yeah. He said you put him up to it.'

Utah started to bristle. Weaver threw him a warning look and jumped in with:

'If a man'd been shot that many times, he'd say anything.'

Madigan smiled thinly. 'He was dying. In a lot of pain. He wanted me to end it for him. I told him I would, providing he told me who put him up to it. Utah Reeves, he said, clear as a bell.'

'You're a goddamn liar!'

Weaver saw he couldn't stop it happening now and he stepped quickly to one side, using his weight to jar Tex Tyrell out of the way as Utah reached for his gun. They both knew Madigan had deliberately prodded the man, forced the showdown.

Utah was mighty fast, his hand a blur as his gun cleared leather and came up, hammer clicking back to full cock, finger depressing the trigger, thumb easing to let the hammer fall. . . .

Madigan's hand dipped and lifted, flame streaking from his fist, and Utah jarred backwards, staggering. His gun fired but the bullet whined harmlessly away. Utah was dead on his feet but he still lifted his smoking gun in one last effort and Madigan coldly shot him through the heart.

All in less than three seconds.

Utah jerked back into Weaver's tent, clawing fingers scratching and tearing at the canvas, pulling it off the frame. It collapsed, billowing, and half-covered Utah's body.

Tex Tyrell had a hand on his gun butt but slowly uncurled his fingers one by one when Madigan's Colt turned in his direction. He shook his head swiftly, pale now; he had decided he wanted no part of this.Whip Weaver was half-crouched, but made sure that Madigan could see his hands were well away from his gun butt.

Madigan holstered his gun and turned to face the men, led by Captain Kerry Bodine himself, coming towards him.

CHAPTER 9

NEW GUN

For some reason, Bodine didn't want to give Madigan a public dressing-down, although he'd sent a man into town for the sheriff.

They were in the captain's tent now: Tyrell, Weaver, Bodine and Madigan, with Lady Anne appearing in the doorway.

Bodine glanced at her but spoke to Madigan.

'I hope you've got a good story for the law, Brennan. You're a damn passel of trouble, feller. I'm beginning to be sorry I hired you on. Word is, was you shot Pancho, too. . . .'

Madigan saw the girl sidling in along one wall, trying to be as inconspicuous as possible.

'Captain, I rode out after the piebald today, a half-broke horse no one in their right mind would take with the intention of riding him or trying to train him for inclusion in some sort of riding act.' He raked cold eyes over Weaver and Tyrell, paused to give either one a chance to reply, but they said nothing. 'The tracks led up to those adobe ruins. Herc was waiting there to bushwhack me.' He touched the bullet hole in the brim of his hat. 'Nearly pulled it off, too.'

'But you killed him,' Bodine said flatly.

'Dunno no other way when someone's trying to blow my head off, Cap. Yeah, I nailed him and he lived for a little while. Told me Utah had set me up.'

'Why the hell would he do that?' Weaver asked quickly, indignant. He looked at Bodine. 'Utah didn't like Brennan, didn't trust him, Cap, but, hell! He wouldn't tell Herc to ambush him!'

'Utah had plenty of guts,' cut in Tyrell bleakly. 'If he'd wanted you dead, he'd have seen to it himself.'

'Backshot me, you mean?'

'Goddamn it to hell, Brennan!' Tyrell was breathing hard and fast through flared nostrils and his right hand jumped a little but it was obvious from the look on his face that he remembered just how fast Madigan had gunned down Utah.

'That's enough!' roared Bodine. 'Tex and Whip have a point, Brennan. Why would Utah want you dead?'

'You'd have to ask him.'

'Is that supposed to be funny?'

'Not from wherever Utah is. Look, I've had a deal of trouble in my life, including that stint in Yuma.' He paused, frowned as Bodine and the others stiffened, looking blank. Madigan started to look towards Lady Anne, but stopped the motion, said quietly: 'I did my time and I'm trying to make some sort of a life for myself now. You gave me a chance, Cap, and I appreciate it.'

'And you show that appreciation by killing my men!'

'If I'm shot at – or called a liar – I'll shoot back every time.' No compromise there, either in tone or attitude, and while Bodine didn't like it, he nodded jerkily.

'I didn't know I was hiring a jailbird, Brennan. But if you've done your time and you do a good job here, why, I guess. . .' he glanced at the tense Weaver and Tyrell, 'I guess I'm willing to give you a break.'

The two rough riders were infuriated by Bodine's words but he gave them a hard look that warned them to keep their mouths shut. They did so, but both men were itching to shout some sort of protest. More so when Bodine added:

'We're now a man short in the *Trio Courageous* act. Think you could do some trick-riding, fill in for Utah in tonight's show? The boys here can train you for more of the act if you pull it off . . .'

'*Judas priest, Cap!*' gritted Weaver, and Tex swore.

Bodine ignored them, awaiting Madigan's answer.

He smiled wryly. 'Reckon I could do it without getting myself killed?'

Bodine knew what he meant and nodded as he turned his gaze on Weaver and Tyrell.

'If you're as good a horseman as I think you are, you'll be all right.'

'There was some mention of extra money if I was called on to do more than wrangling and black-smithing,' Madigan reminded him.

Bodine smiled crookedly: he thought he had found the chink in Madigan's armour now.

'That can be arranged. But you give me tonight, gratis, and if it's satisfactory we'll work something out about money.'

'Suits me. Thanks, Captain.'

Madigan hitched at his gun belt and nodded curtly to the silent woman as he left the tent.

'Why the hell you keeping that son of a bitch around, Cap?' demanded Whip Weaver. 'You can't trust him!'

'And he's a jailbird to boot,' growled Tyrell.

Bodine glanced at Lady Anne as he said heavily; 'Yeah. So I learned. Eventually!'

Before he could say more she moved out of the tent. He seemed as if he would call her back but changed his mind.

'Well, Cap?' Weaver said, still angry. 'Why we gotta work with Brennan?'

'Because it's better to have the son of a bitch here where we can see him, watch what he's doing – if he's doing anything, and I'm yet to be convinced of that. Personally, I think he's one tough *hombre* and Utah went off half-cocked trying to fix it so Herc could bushwhack him.'

'Well. Being able to watch him could be a good thing, I guess,' Weaver admitted slowly.

'Yeah?' snapped Tyrell. 'Well, I'll watch the bastard, all right! He won't be able to spit without me seeing him do it.'

'Best start figuring out something for him to do tonight. Something he can manage easily.' Bodine flicked his eyes from one man to the other. 'If we do have reason to want him out of the way permanently, an "accident" can be arranged, timed to take place before a full audience. Not only will it exonerate us, but the publicity will do us a helluva lot of good, I shouldn't be surprised.'

'And save us some money,' Weaver said.

All three of them grinned at that.

Then Bodine said, smile fading: 'Speaking of money . . .'

He watched them expectantly, waiting.

'So you never told our captain about those prison papers.'

Lady Anne, on her way back to her tent, jumped and whirled as Madigan stepped out from between two tents. Her hand went to her belt and he saw the glint of polished metal. She smiled crookedly.

'Jumpy, huh?'

'You like to flirt with danger, I think, Brennan!' She did not remove her hand from the butt of the small gun in her belt. 'No, I didn't tell Captain Bodine about your prison papers. From the look on his face, I think I should have . . .' Her voice was a little uncertain with regret. 'I don't know why I didn't tell him. Perhaps – perhaps I thought that if you'd served your time, you deserved a chance to make good.'

His smile widened, but there was little genuine pleasure in it.

'Of course you did.'

Her eyes narrowed. 'There's not a lot of gratitude

in your make-up, is there, Brennan!'

'Maybe you'd be surprised what is there,' he replied and left her puzzling over the remark.

They worked out what they figured to be a simple routine for Madigan in the *Trio* part of the show – but it contained more than an element of danger and he knew it right from the start. He had been expecting it and wasn't disappointed.

'You said you spent a heap of time with Indians over the years,' Whip Weaver told him with a hint of aggression in his voice that would have warned Madigan in any case. 'Said you went on buffalo hunts, shooting from the saddle. . . ?'

It was a query and Madigan merely nodded. Tex Tyrell was standing by, trying to hide a smirk, arms folded.

'OK. Then you ought to be able to slip over the horse's rump at full gallop, hang on to his tail and swing alongside, then jump back on. I know it's pretty basic but we haven't time for anything fancy.'

'Basic? I reckon it's the kind of thing you learn only after years of practice.'

'Scared to try?' asked Tyrell, chuckling.

'I'll *do* it, not try. Just letting you heroes know that I'm not as green as you figure. I'll even take a sideways jump, hang on to the stirrup, let the horse drag me under his belly, grab the opposite stirrup, then come up on the other side and jump back into the saddle.'

That stopped them for a moment or two. Then Weaver, sober and cold-eyed, said:

'Fine. But that's a mite more than basic.'

'Hell, let him try, Whip, man knows what he's doing. Or thinks he does. By the by, you know we won't lose any sleep if you don't pull it off.'

'Never figured you would. You want me in on the rescue act, saving the stage passengers from the Indians?'

'Sure. Incorporate those tricks we just talked about . . . if you figure you can pull 'em off.'

'Kind of rusty, but I'll manage.'

'Not much time before the show,' Tyrell pointed out cheerfully. 'For rehearsals.'

'That's OK. I'll do it cold.'

'Ker-riiist! But you sure have got confidence, ain't you!' Weaver said, shaking his head.

'Just figured this was the big boys' time, let the sap flow, show you got real *cojones* – all that kinda crap you two seem to favour.'

They didn't like it but Tyrell gave Madigan a crooked smile.

'Better keep clear of *our* horses.'

'Aim to. And you *heeroes* better keep clear of me. If I'm crowded and it's too late to stop, you can bet at least one of you'll go down with me – that ought to make the audience jump to their feet. You'll get 'em coming back again and again. Nothing like a fatal pile-up to drag 'em back.'

Their smirks disappeared and Madigan went to the corrals, took down a rope and stepped through the rails, walking casually through the slowly milling horses. Eventually he selected a palomino.

'Hey, that was Utah's!' snapped Tyrell, who had

followed him and was in the act of climbing the rails.

'Now it's mine. Why don't you go get into your fancy outfit, Tex? Time's running out – for all of us.'

As Madigan began gentling the palomino, Tyrell climbed down slowly, frowning.

Just what the hell did Madigan mean – all of us?

Everyone and his brother from the town was there at the arena, plus all the folk who had ridden in from miles around. They cheered and stomped and threw their hats into the air, especially after the *Trio Courageous* act. Madigan had proved to be as agile and 'courageous' as the act required. There were still plenty of empty seats, though, but Captain Bodine didn't seem to be worried. In fact, he looked – and was – a happy man, grinning around his cigarillo and wearing his fringed buckskin outfit. He leaned on a gatepost as he watched the crowd cheering Lady Anne when she stood up on the specially made saddle and shot the coloured feathers from the Indian dream-catcher atop a high pole as her horse galloped flat out.

Didn't matter that it wasn't a full house, Kerry Bodine told himself, mellowed some by a few bonded bourbons. Didn't matter at *all*! Not after what the *Trio* had brought back from the Castle Peak Bank. They hadn't had time to count it yet, but the sheriff had told him, after he'd cleared Madigan of any wrongdoing in the killings of Hercules and Utah, that three robbers had stolen the best part of $52,000 in Castle Peak. Five townsmen were dead and some others wounded, but he didn't know how many and there was a big manhunt on back beyond Chino Pass, many miles away.

Captain Bodine didn't care about the manhunt.

Hell, fifty-two grand was the biggest-ever bag of loot. He had been going to make it their last job for some time, didn't want to push his luck. But he'd learned about a train leaving Creede for Alamosa with an express car full of gold ingots from the Creede mines – worth at least $100,000 – bound eventually for the Denver mint.

He was always a man who believed in riding the wave of success until it dwindled to a trickle.

It would be dangerous, but it could be the last job they'd ever need to do if they could pull it off.

Of course they could! They'd never missed yet!

They would need at least one other man, though, but he reckoned Brennan could be bought cheap: the man was turning out a hell of a lot better than he'd figured. Had done that trick-riding earlier without a hitch, and Captain Bodine had been feeling so good by that time that he'd asked Brennan if he would care to try the *Runaway Stage* act as he himself was feeling a mite poorly and not quite up to it. . . ?

Brennan had jumped at the chance, but he'd held up Bodine for a lousy hundred-dollar fee. Luckily Bodine had the bourbon warming his belly by that time and had agreed. Tyrell and Weaver, of course, were peeved at first, but after giving it a little thought, grinned, feeling sure Brennan was a goner, attempting the runaway stage rescue cold-turkey. . . .

Were they surprised! Fact was, Bodine was surprised himself at how effortlessly Brennan made that jump from the racing horse on to the side of the stage, clambered up on top, dropped into the driving-seat and then down on to the swinging wagon-tongue swaying and leaping between the thundering horses so as to retrieve the flying reins. In the end, he had *walked* along that damn swaying, jarring beam right down to the lead horses who had ears laid flat and manes flying. He leapt on to the back of the right-side leader and twisted hell out of its ears until it slowed, then he'd changed grip to the bridle and hauled the stage up in a cloud of dust right smack in front of the dress-circle seats, giving them the best view possible. The crowd cheered itself hoarse.

Bit of a maverick, but game as they come, that Bronco Brennan, Bodine allowed after the first surprise had worn off. That was when he decided to put it to Brennan to come join their group – and grow rich. Fast.

Well, sort of put it to him.

They were in Bodine's tent, drinking Bodine's fine whiskey. They saluted each other and sipped – it was too mellow to toss down quickly.

'You did good, Bronco.'

'Gonna suffer for it in the morning,' Madigan said, easing around in the canvas chair. 'The old bones tend to feel it more than they did twenty years ago.'

'Don't I know it!' Bodine agreed, laughing. 'There'll be one performance at noon and then we pack up and move on.'

Madigan moaned. 'Never like moving camp more

often than I have to. I carry as little gear as I can get by with. Just enough to fill my war bag.'

Bodine looked at him sharply. 'Yeah, I had you figured for a loner. Something about you, Brennan. Dunno whether I like it or not. Whip and Tex sure don't.'

'Because I killed Utah.'

'*And* outrode them at their own game. What I wanted to talk to you about – you did time in Yuma. What for?'

Madigan shrugged. 'They picked me up for murder and robbery, but couldn't make the murder charge stick.'

'What did you rob?' Bodine tried to sound casual, but he was eager to hear this.

'Bank – and a paytrain on its way to the mines in the Superstition Mountains. A guard fell off his horse, hit his head on a rock and died. Sheriff reckoned it was murder because if I hadn't jumped the paytrain the guard wouldn't've fallen while trying to get at his shotgun. Fool ought've been carrying it cocked and ready, anyway.'

Bodine gave a suggestion of a smile. 'You say pay*train*. You mean an actual train?'

Madigan shook his head. 'Three guards on horses, leading a line of pack-mules. Was supposed to be a normal supply delivery, but I heard there was a payroll hidden amongst the coffee and flour and sowbelly. I was too greedy, though. I'd just got a thousand from the bank and was on my way to Mexico, but figured I might's well try for early retirement and went for the payroll.'

'How'd you get caught?'

Madigan sighed. 'Hate to say it – was a bright-eyed *señorita*. Turned me in for a reward. Figured she'd seen me making eyes at another feller's gal.'

'Of course, you weren't!'

'We-ell, I might've been. None too sure myself. It was mighty good tequila we were drinking . . .'

Bodine laughed. 'Just bad luck.'

'That's how I look at it. You got what you wanted?'

Bodine shook his head slowly. 'You're not as dumb as you act, Brennan, and I *know* I ought to be a little more leery of you than I am, but – I can't afford to pass up a certain . . . opportunity. And you did leave me a man short.'

'Thought I'd replaced him. If you mean Utah.'

'In the show, I guess you have. But we've got another kind of show going, the boys and me . . .'

Madigan frowned, indicated his empty glass but Bodine didn't want any more bourbon clouding his judgement, so he shook his head.

'Maybe later. You interested?'

'I dunno what to be interested in yet.'

'I tell you, you better had be interested – or you don't walk out of this tent alive.'

Madigan didn't react much, just looked around casually, a mixture of query and open contempt.

'Just take my word for it, Brennan. You want me to go on?'

'Sounds like there's money somewhere and I told you once, money *always* gets my attention.'

'That's what I figured.' Bodine looked a little more relaxed now. 'This – deal we have. I'm not

109

going into details. I don't trust you – or my judgement at the moment – that much. But here's an
outline. You've heard of all those bank robberies
here and there all round the country? Not just this
state, I mean others, too.'

Madigan frowned. 'Seems I have. Took a kind of –
professional interest, I guess, but there weren't many
details. Two, usually three, fellers, sometimes even
four, I heard, counting the one who brought up the
horses. Straight hold-up once or twice, a few times
they got in the back of the bank somehow, couple
others they took the family of the banker hostage.
Dunno if the law figured it was just one gang, 'cause
it was just that little bit different each time. But I had
a notion it was just one bunch doing it.'

'Unfortunately, I've had word passed along to me
that the US marshals think the same thing. Texas
Rangers, too. So, we're feeling a little jumpy, you
see.'

Madigan deliberately arched his eyebrows. 'You're
saying you and those – *heroes* – are behind it?'

'I admit to nothing, but listen to this scenario. A
travelling medicine show, or perhaps even a show
like this one, moves all over the country, towns far
apart, law scattered, of course, most towns with banks
busting at the seams because they can't transfer their
cash just by snapping their fingers. They have to wait
for armed escorts, or an army patrol, or a secure
express car on a train.'

'Hmmm. Hadn't looked at it that way. Any bank I
robbed was just some piss-ant job I pulled. Never
worried about the safes, just got what I could from

the clerks and vamoosed pronto.'

Bodine smiled crookedly. 'Then you're not quite as smart as I thought. Worthwhile targets make any risk worthwhile. A travelling show like ours can move around virtually anywhere we want to, never under suspicion of anything more lawless than buying a couple of cows to feed the crew without a bill of sale. Get the idea?'

'Sure. People who make other people happy usually aren't suspected of anything bad, 'specially something like robbery and murder.'

'Uh-huh. And 'specially if they're a long way from where the robbery takes place.'

'But still close enough for the expert riders to hightail it back to a town the show's been to earlier. And while you were there entertaining, you'd've found out all you needed to know about the bank: how much it carries, the routine for moving cash around, and so on.'

Bodine remained silent for a time, studying Madigan. He spoke slowly. 'I – don't know about you, Brennan. Maybe you're just a mite *too* quick on the uptake.'

Madigan shrugged. 'Just enthusiastic, is all. I like your idea. You don't have to go into any more detail. I'd guess Herc was the one who made sure the getaway mounts were where they were supposed to be. But you fired him.'

'Had to – thanks to you. You showed him up for a fool in front of a lot of people, you beat him in a fight. Then he sassed Whip and Whip would never take any back-talk from Herc so he told him to draw his time. I had to go along with him then, had to stand by one of the stars of the show. But Herc was always a sore loser and Utah didn't trust you anyway – they were blood-kin, you know. They set it up, made a try for you up at the ruins. Just them two, nothing to do with the rest of us. You proved too good for 'em, and I reckon you've proved yourself in lots of ways since, Bronco, so I'm taking a chance with you now.'

'You're cutting me in on your special deal?' Madigan sounded suspicious and he was, but it was also what Bodine would expect. 'Or still just considering it?'

The captain spread his hands.

'Cutting you in? Special deal?' He shook his head. 'I'm just offering you a riding job as part of the *Trio*. This other thing, why, I'm just talking about what *might* happen if men from a show like this took it into their heads to get rich the fast way.'

'Well, in theory, I reckon I'd be interested if anyone offered me a deal like that. The years are passing way too fast lately.'

Bodine laughed, stood up, went to his bottle on the small portable table and filled both glasses to the brim.

'Well, that's worth another drink, I reckon. The years come and the years go, and they go a damn sight faster'n they come! Let's drink to – what shall it be? Enjoying those years left to us, to the full?'

'Sounds good.' Madigan raised his glass and drank, smacked his lips, then stood stiffly. 'I'd best turn in if we have another show tomorrow.' He paused at the tent flap. 'You can let me know if you want my help with anything else that comes up, eh? Theoretical or otherwise.'

Bodine nodded and Madigan stepped outside, spun quickly when he saw a dark outline, sixgun making a slight sound as it cleared leather and the hammer cocked back.

'Judas priest!' exclaimed Tex Tyrell, backing up, the sawn-off shotgun he held forgotten, startled at the speed of Madigan's draw.

Madigan saw the gun and slashed at the man's wrist, knocking the weapon free. It thudded on the ground as Tyrell howled, clasped his numbed hand to his chest. 'You won't be needing that now, Tex.'

Tyrell was still too stunned to speak and he watched, his eyes wide, rubbing his numbed wrist, as Madigan moved off, holstering his Colt. He was surprised to realize he was shaking.

Madigan glanced back once and thought he saw someone else moving in the deeper shadow behind Bodine's tent.

Likely Weaver; both he and Tyrell would have been listening outside the tent, hoping he would do or say something stupid so they'd have an excuse to take him out into the night and blow his brains out.

Not right now, fellers. But maybe after I've done all that Cap wants me to you'll make your try.

'And maybe I'll be ready for you,' he murmured as he entered his tent. 'Hell! I'd *better* be!'

CHAPTER 10

MOVING ON

Madigan was sitting on the edge of his bedroll, grunting as he pulled off his boots, when he heard someone at the tent flap. He rolled swiftly, snatching up the unholstered Colt, quickly covering the door.

Lady Anne Little froze in the doorway, her arms full of towels and holding a bottle of liniment or oil. She was still wearing her showtime outfit except for the vest and gloves and the blonde wig. She released a breath and shook her head slightly as she came in, the flap falling back into place behind her.

'I don't believe I've ever seen anyone as edgy as you, Bronco. Nor, for that matter, as quick on the draw.'

'Keeps me alive – both things.'

She looked at him soberly as she knelt beside the bedroll. He frowned as she laid out the towels and the bottle.

'Take off your shirt.' she told him as she poured a

little oil into one cupped hand and began to rub her hands together. 'I'll give you a massage.'

He stared at her.

She smiled, chuckled. 'After all those acrobatics on your horse you surely must be a mass of aches.'

'Not yet, I'm not. Kind of stiff, but—'

'You'll be like a board by morning if you don't let me knead those muscles and relax them. Come on. I've seen you with more than your shirt off, remember.'

If she expected him to blush she was disappointed. He unbuttoned his shirt and took it off, lying face down on the towel he spread over his bedroll at her instructions.

'I haven't see you with your shirt off.'

'And you're not likely to.' Her fingers dug into his knotted shoulder muscles and he couldn't quite smother the grunt of pain.

Then the fingertips manipulated and kneaded and caressed his muscles all the way down from his shoulders to his waist, both sides of his spine, the back of his neck and up the occipital bulge of his skull. Despite his decision to remain alert, he felt himself relaxing, drifting into sleep. But he blinked, shook his head, brought himself back.

'Don't do that,' she admonished lightly. 'Let yourself go, fall into a restful sleep.'

'I'm OK,' he told her stubbornly.

She sighed. 'You must live a very stressful life, Bronco Brennan. It's not good for you.'

'Trying to reform me?' He rolled on to his side and she sat back on her heels, frowning, hand still

115

oily, fingers spread, ready to continue massaging. 'Look, thanks for doing this. I feel good. But that's enough. I don't let anyone put me to sleep.' He saw the hurt flare in her eyes and knew he was being unreasonable, forced a crooked grin. 'Especially if they're trying to do it with a gun butt.'

But her face remained sober and she wiped her hands on a small towel.

'Well, you're bound to feel some benefit. Why're you so hostile, Bronco? So – suspicious of people?'

'I ride the edge of the law. Learned a long time ago not to trust anyone. Sorry, but that's just the way I am.'

'And it's "take it or leave it", isn't it?' There was bitterness in her tone as she began to gather her things.

He nodded gently, holding his gaze to her stiff face.

'You once said you thought I'm a dangerous man. Well, I am. And I'm *in* danger lots of the time, too. Nothing personal in me being suspicious. Just self-preservation.'

She relaxed a little, nodded as she gave him a tiny smile. 'I guess I'm not used to men like you.'

She started to rise and he reached out, held her slim wrist, felt her sudden tension as she tried to pull free.

'What kind of men are you used to? Men who wear dinner suits, big, curly wigs, silk-brocade waistcoats?'

'I think you've been reading too much of the more romantic fiction about English people!'

He released her, said nothing for a moment, yet

116

she didn't make any move to go.

Then he said quietly: 'I don't think you've ever seen England.'

She stiffened and quickly stood up. 'What're you talking about? I was *born* there!'

'I doubt it.' He stood, flexing his arms and shoulders, pulled on his shirt, eyes seeking hers – and they were blazing back at him. 'That's a North Texas accent you're trying to hide there under all the la-de-da or I'm the ghost of General Custer.'

Her mouth had shrunk to a tight little rose and her eyes were slitted. 'You're mad!'

He grinned. 'Hey! That was a real first-class imitation of an indignant Limey! But you still haven't convinced me. What's your name?'

'You know it's Anne Little!'

'I know that's your stage name. Your real one's likely to be something like Mary-Jo Huckerbee. Or' – he fluttered his eyelashes and simpered, speaking in an exagerrated Texas accent – 'Missy Magnolia, Ah do de-clare!'

She almost burst out laughing despite herself, tried hard to cover but unsuccessfully.

'Oh, your accent is worse than mine! That was *terrible*! If they heard you speak like that down home they'd ride you out of town on a rail!'

His grin widened and he shrugged. 'Just where is down home?'

She thought about answering for quite some time.

'You wouldn't know it. A little place called Channing. It's—'

'Just north of Amarillo. I've been there. And I was

117

right about North Texas, eh?'

'You've *been* there? When?'

'Two, three years ago. After the edge of that twister went through, scattered most of the town to hell and gone. Recollect seeing the sign from Pennyfeather's Livery caught up in a Joshua tree nigh on ten miles out of town.'

She seemed more wary now. 'So you really were there.'

He remained silent and then she said abruptly: 'My name's Charity Fletcher.'

'Could be Limey at that! Why try to hide it?'

'As you said, the "Lady Anne" thing is just a stage name. It draws people, thinking I'm a real live English aristocrat.' She seemed uncomfortable under his enquiring stare. '*Now* what's bothering you?'

'You need to watch your accent. Not only doesn't sound quite right to me, but it slips all over the place.'

'Yes, I know. I – I get tired of it but Cap insists I use it all the time: "cultivate" it, he says, make it sound "real".' She laughed shortly. 'The only "English" accent I've ever heard was when a music-hall comedian recited a poem about "Lady Muck and Bassingdale's Duck" and assured everyone that that was how an English gentlewoman would speak. No one in Channing knew the difference ... and nobody else has noticed anything wrong with my version before now.'

'Well then, that's OK, I guess.' But there was something in his tone that made her think that he didn't *quite* believe her. It made her mad but she tried not to show it.

'It's nice to have your approval!' she snapped.

'No skin off my nose. You have to do what the captain tells you, anyway, I guess. He's in charge, right?'

She started to say something, stopped, then said: 'We all have to do as he says – including you, Brennan!'

'Long as I get paid on time, I don't care.'

'Are you really that – that interested in money?'

'Aren't you? I mean, he'd have to pay you more than five bucks a week for you to risk your neck doing that act of yours. If you weren't interested in big money, you'd just walk away and get a job behind a store counter, or marry some hardrock rancher and surround yourself with a handful of kids hanging on your skirts.'

'What d'you know about it!' she demanded, tight-lipped. 'Just what the hell do you know about *anything* connected with me! Now, get out of my way!'

She swept past him, almost knocking him down as she wrenched open the tent flap and stormed out into the night.

He stood in the doorway, holding up the flap, watching her stride angrily towards her own tent.

'I know you can shoot mighty straight – and I wish I knew a lot more about you. *A hell of a lot more.*'

He added this last as she abruptly veered away from her own tent and went into Captain Kerry Bodine's instead.

Chaos ruled again. Madigan was damned if he knew

which was worse, setting up the huge arena and the seats and corrals and tents, or pulling everything down, packing it on to the mules and moving on.

Either way, he didn't care much for this kind of life. But pretty soon now he would have all the evidence he needed to nail Captain Kerry Bodine and his *Trio Courageous*. His hunches were working overtime, too. Bodine seemed easy-going, happy now, he supposed, with what the *Trio* had pulled off in Castle Peak – rumours were flying that the killers had gotten away with $100,000 but he doubted it was that much. Still, there was a cold kind of ruthlessness showing behind the captain's eyes, and it was there even when he was laughing and pouring a drink to toast your health or success to the Wild West Show.

Tex Tyrell and Whip Weaver would kill him as soon as they got a chance – or Bodine OK'd it. 'Lady' Anne? Well, she was a bit of a mystery: seemed interested in him, but had a flash of temper that could be more than just wanting to slap a man's face for riling her. Maybe she was used to shooting off her guns so much – she had to practise constantly to keep up that standard of accuracy – that what she'd really like to do when her dander was up was put a bullet in whoever had upset her.

But one thing he had to admit: she sure knew how to take the kinks out of a man's muscles. He was truly surprised at how supple and relaxed he felt when he rolled out of his bedroll, washed up at the stream and went for breakfast.

'You're moving well,' Lady Anne remarked, sitting down on the log beside him, holding a tin platter of bacon and eggs and beans and a mug of coffee.

'Thanks to you.' He nodded to her meal. 'A "lady" ought to have her breakfast in her tent instead of with the peasants, shouldn't she? Keep up appearances and all that. . . .'

There! There was that near-murderous flash in her eyes, a slight twitch that tightened her lips.

'Are you trying to be funny?'

'Matter of fact, yeah.'

'Oh. Well, if you bothered to look around you would see that my tent is more than half-way dismantled already – by some of those "peasants" you mentioned.'

He sighed, draining his coffee. 'OK. Well, I guess that's the end of this conversation. I'll go see if I can find Cliff and Bobcat somewhere. *Adios,* for now.'

She watched him stroll down to the stream and wash his platter and mug, deposit them near the chuckwagon, which was almost packed and ready to roll. The cook was crankily cussing and kicking pans and the odd crew member who happened to be in range of his boot. Madigan grinned to himself: someone else who hated the trail move.

Madigan didn't glance in her direction again, called to Cliff and Bobcat where they were smoking with a few idle hands and started down towards the corrals.

He heard a *whooshing* sound and had begun to turn when something stinging coiled around his legs, jerked hard, and next thing he was spitting dirt and lifting his face out of the dust. He shook his head and was aware that Cliff and Bobcat were running up with

121

the idlers and then whatever was pinning his legs tightened and he was dragged brutally backwards, belly down, across the gravel.

He rolled on to his back and saw the trouble. Tyrell was moving in on him while Weaver kept tension on the bullwhip he had lashed around Madigan's legs. Tex Tyrell seemed to favour his right hand and Madigan even got a glimpse of swollen and bruised flesh – and knew the roughrider was about to pay him back for rapping him with his gun barrel last night.

He tried to fight his legs free of the whip, but Weaver was expert with the bullwhip and kept the tension on, holding the coils tight. Tyrell curled a lip as he ran in and drove a boot into Madigan's side. The marshal tried to hunch up but Weaver made sure he couldn't pull his legs up to his chest to give him any kind of protection. Tyrell kicked again – and again.

'You son of a bitch! Figure you can come in here and ride roughshod over everyone! Sucking up to the captain, even to Lady Anne! Well, Cap might not know it yet, but he's gonna be short a wrangler. You ain't gonna be able to sit a horse for a looooooooooong time, mister!'

Madigan rolled violently as the boot swung again and then Bobcat was charging in, Cliff alongside, and they roughhoused Tyrell aside so that the man staggered wildly, fighting for balance.

'Give him a break, you yallerbelly!' snarled Cliff, shoving Tyrell hard on the shoulder, sending the man stumbling again.

Bobcat stepped in between Cliff and the savagely angry Tyrell who was reaching for his gun.

'Don't do that!' Bobcat drawled and Tyrell froze when he saw the sixgun pointing at him, rock-steady in Bobcat's gloved hand.

Weaver's attention had been distracted by the interference of the trail men and the whip loosened, the lash sagging. Madigan sat up, grabbed the whip and yanked hard, pulling it out of Weaver's grip. The man stumbled and by then Madigan had the coils free of his legs. He scrambled up, swung the whip as he straightened, and the heavy, shot-loaded butt took Weaver across the side of the head. The man's feet left the ground and he fell, dazed, trying to push up. Madigan stepped in and kicked him in the head. He reversed his hold on the long bullwhip and Tyrell threw up an arm, anticipating what was coming next.

Madigan swung the whip as the man cried out and turned to run. He snapped his arm back and the lash cracked like a pistol shot and slashed Tyrell's shirt clear across his shoulders, breaking the flesh. Tex yelled and stumbled wildly, putting down his hands to keep from falling all the way. His swollen hand twisted under his weight and he spilled sideways to the ground where he cowered. Madigan stood above him, coiling the whip casually, his face granite-hard.

'Don't – whip – me!' Tyrell gasped. Although it was a plea, there was a touch of a threat there, too.

Madigan smiled, the whip coiled now. He swung back-handed and the supple coils of plaited leather, heavy now that they were all lying together, took Tex Tyrell in the face. The leather ripped and tore his flesh, wrenching a nostril and his upper lip into blood-gushing gashes, mauling upwards and tearing loose one eyebrow, sliding across to mash the tip of an ear, which turned purple and began to swell almost immediately. Tyrell sprawled, sobbing in pain, drawing up his legs, huddled, tensed as he waited for more.

Madigan flung the whip on to his quivering body, leaned down and flung the man on to his back. Tyrell stared up wide-eyed from his bloody, disfigured face. Madigan smiled and it twisted Tex's guts like nothing else had done so far.

'Next time, I'll tear your head clear off your shoulders.' He pushed Tyrell back contemptuously and straightened, turning to Cliff and Bobcat. 'Thanks, boys. You've earned yourself a bonus.'

Surprisingly they shook their heads and Cliff drawled: 'Not for goin' agin scum like that.' He spat on the groggy Weaver's boots.

Madigan nodded. 'We've got a trail drive ahead of us. Get your gear and we'll round up the horses, and get a head start. Those pack-mules will slow us down otherwise.'

The prospect of trail-driving seemed to please the two rannies and they hurried off, grinning. The crew who had come a-running when the fight had started looked wearily at Madigan and his gaze touched that of Lady Anne.

'You were right,' she told him quietly and soberly 'You *are* a dangerous man, Bronco Brennan! *Very* dangerous.'

'Have my moments,' he said and then Captain

Bodine stepped in front of him and said curtly:

'My tent. Right away.' The showman heeled and strode angrily towards his tent which was still standing, although most of the others had already been struck.

Madigan paused to rub some circulation back into his lower legs which were ridged from the whip's coils, grimaced as he straightened and pressed one hand into his throbbing side as he moved up to Bodine's tent, wanting a cigarette badly.

The captain was waiting, tapping fingers against the edge of his portable table, which contained the bottles of bourbon and glasses.

'By hell, Bronco! What're you trying to do? Put me out of action?'

'Never laid a finger on you as I recollect.'

Bodine's face coloured darkly. 'Don't get frisky with me, damn you! You know how I need Tex and Whip! Now look what you've done to them!'

Madigan silently pulled up the legs of his trousers and let Bodine see the red, swelling welts left by the whip's coils. Two were oozing a little blood. He pulled up his shirt, showed the red marks and torn skin from Tyrell's boots.

Bodine sighed. 'Aw, shooot! Damned if I know what to do with you fellers! Hate each other's guts! Well, you're all gonna have to bite down on the bit until this deal's over.'

'Tell your boys, Captain.'

'Don't worry, I will.' He turned to pour a glass of bourbon each, handed one to Madigan. ' 'Luck, Bronco. We're all going to need it – now.'

Madigan drank without acknowledging the toast.

'I've sold off most of the horses,' Bodine said abruptly and as Madigan began a question, added: 'Not the ones that're trained for the show – the others are those we usually pick up at each stop, just for the stampede and round-up scenes, you know 'em.'

'Want us to cut out the show broncs, then.'

'Yes. But I sold the others to a ranch in the San Juans, Broken J, run by a feller calls himself Hi-spade Billy Chandler. He'll take the broncs but he wants 'em delivered to his spread. So you pick a couple of hands. Bobcat and Cliff oughta do, might keep 'em outta trouble down here, and they're both trail men, anyway. You three drive the horses up there, taking your own mounts with you – you're the only one can ride that piebald, anyway. Seem to make a good team, you and that outlaw.'

Madigan seemed suddenly exasperated.

'Look, Cap, not long ago you had me in here, feeding me some eyewash about joining your group for some easy pickings. Now we're talking about me driving horses up into the mountains. Way I savvied things, after this big deal you reckon you're cooking up, a man could retire. I just wish to hell you'd make up your mind what you want me to do.'

Bodine swung around from reaching for the bourbon bottle, his eyes blazing.

'I can soon damn make up my mind to fire you – right here and now!'

'Well, for Chris'sake do something. Stop this pissing me around so I don't know whether I'm coming or going.'

Madigan was deliberately pushing: he needed more details.

Bodine still didn't like Madigan's attitude but it was clear he was fighting down his urge to break into a rage, treading warily here, figuring Madigan was deadly and a lot more dangerous that he had demonstrated so far.

'All right. I admit things likely seem confused right now. But I need you for this chore, Bronco. After that, you get your share and we go our separate ways.'

That was what Madigan wanted to know: Bodine needed him right now.

'Share of what?' he asked unbending.

'Whatever's in the express car on that train.'

'Judas! *What* train we talking about?'

Bodine regarded him coolly. 'The one we're using to move the show to Alamosa. We'll pack up here and drive the mules up through Dolomite Pass and pick it up at Del Norte. But you're going to deliver those horses to Broken J then, with Bobcat and Cliff, you'll meet the train at Buckskin Ridge with our getaway mounts – all three of you wearing those long rubber slickers I supply to the crew for wet weather.' Bodine smiled faintly. 'Could put as much as twenty thousand dollars in your pocket, Bronco. How's that sound?'

Bodine's expression said plainly he figured that that amount would knock Madigan clear out of his boots – he had him put down as small-time, a man who would figure $20,000 was a fortune he could retire on. So Madigan reckoned he'd better not disillusion him.

He whistled softly. 'Much as that!' And he saw the smirk on Bodine's face swiftly erased as the man forced a smile. 'But why do we have to wear those goddamn hot slickers? You expecting rain?'

Bodine shook his head, smiling slightly.

'You wear them so we know it's *you* and not some blamed posse trying to drop a noose over our heads.'

There were warning bells clanging insanely in Madigan's head, but somehow he managed just to keep a mildly surprised look on his face. Play it dumb and learn a lot more – hopefully!

Or die for being too dumb.

Lying awake in his bedroll under the stars – he had pulled down his tent as it was a fine starry night – Madigan thought he had it figured.

A blind man could see Bodine and his men aimed to rob that express car, at the point of a blazing gun if necessary. But they didn't trust *him* enough to take him in on that part of the deal. They would leave the train at Buckskin Ridge. That was why Bodine wanted Madigan and the two young trail riders waiting there with the getaway horses.

OK. It was possible, *just* possible, that he might get some kind of a share that was gold and not lead, but he figured on the latter. And would be ready for it. Trouble was, what was going to happen to Bobcat and Cliff?

He owed them plenty. They were young rannies, a bit reckless, but essentially fun-loving and out for a bit of healthy hell-raising. They had years ahead of them and all the good things that time could hold. He didn't aim for anyone to cut them dead – literally – even if he blew the assignment keeping them alive.

At the same time he didn't want to warn them too far ahead. Especially Cliff. Couple of beers or redeyes and he was willing – and eager – to take on the whole blame world, and if it was wearing a tin star so much the better.

So, he made his decision: they would drive the horses to Broken J and then he would pay them off out of his own pocket, tell them to vamoose, and he would deliver the getaway mounts to this Buckskin Ridge alone. That would keep them out of trouble.

That was his plan, anyway.

CHAPTER 11

OVER THE SAN JUANS

Madigan caught a glimpse of Tex Tyrell as he and Bobcat and Cliff drove out the bunch of horses. There was no mistaking the man – he had bandages slanting across his face, the white splotched with blood, and he was moving slowly. One eye was completely visible, the other with ripped eyebrow, about half-visible.

There was hatred and the urge to murder in both eyes. Madigan gave him a perfunctory salute as he rode by and Tyrell dropped a hand to gun butt. Weaver, standing beside him and looking just as menacing, stopped him, shaking his head. Tyrell pulled his hand away irritably.

'You'll keep, Brennan!' he called hoarsely.

Madigan saw Lady Anne standing near the chuckwagon and he waved, but she did not wave back. He shrugged.

Bobcat and Cliff were riding easily, at home with this kind of chore, eager to shake the restrictions of the show camp, looking forward to their wages and the pleasures they would buy.

It was a long drive and the easy part was across the flats to the foothills of the San Juans. The piebald was along and they kept it in the midst of the bunch as much as possible. There was still that roving eye as it examined the wild places it no doubt preferred to the confines of the corral and the company of the broken-in horses.

Behind, the captain would be breaking camp and starting the long haul with the pack-mule team and the wagons carrying all the show's gear. It would be a long, tiring drive and everyone would be glad to get aboard the train at Del Norte. Bodine had arranged for two special cars for the use of his crew and himself, and six flatbed wagons for carrying the gear – tents, poles, gates, huge rolls of painted canvas backdrops and all the tools – would be waiting at Del Norte for loading. By the time the train arrived from Creede they would be ready to hitch on.

Normally the train was scheduled to make a fast run down to Alamosa and then on, eventually, to Denver, but no railroad could afford to refuse passage and freight gear to Captain Bodine's Wild West Show. It was becoming famous, and a good deal of money was involved in the renting of rolling stock to Bodine's outfit.

The express car carrying the gold would be

hitched on and the train would start its long, long journey, slowed way down by now with the extra weight. . . .

Madigan had tried his best to learn what the train was carrying that made it so valuable but Bodine refused to tell him, talked all around the subject and kept dangling the promised $20,000 like a glittering prize. Madigan didn't push too hard, but did some griping, because he knew that would be expected. But it wasn't hard to figure what was on that train, coming as it was from gold-mining country up around Creede. What really worried him was that he wouldn't be on the train to prevent the actual hold-up.

It had been a smart move of Bodine's, sending him up into the San Juans with the horses, keeping him right away from telegraph lines or the law. Just in case. . . . After all, it would be the first time Bodine had used Madigan and if this was to be as big a deal as the captain claimed, he would want to make as much use of Madigan as possible without giving him a chance to pull any kind of a double-cross.

Madigan's only plan now was to dump these horses fast at Hi-spade Chandler's spread and arrive early at the rendezvous, leave Bobcat and Cliff with the getaway mounts and then hightail it downtrack and get aboard the train much earlier than Bodine or the others expected. He couldn't stand by idly while the express car guards were killed.

This gang had a reputation for murder of almost anyone within gunshot and he didn't aim to allow it to happen this time.

*

The show pack-train would be using Dolomite Pass through the San Juan mountains but Madigan and his men had no such short cut. They had to swing north and then north-west and do a switchback on a high trail that was thankfully quite wide, then run the ridges to the east.

Up here was more or less the 'back' of the San Juans and it towered above cattle country used by many of the ranches. Hi-spade Billy Chandler had gone one better and built his spread on the ridges, utilizing the grassy benches and the flatland between for grazing his cattle. He seemed to be having a deal of success, for the scatttered cows that Madigan and his crew saw were well fed and had plenty of meat on their bones. They came across one lone cowboy who regarded them suspiciously, unsheathed his rifle and levered in a shell before holding it with the butt on his thigh and a finger through the trigger-guard.

He was unshaven, dirty, a typical line-shacker who was happy to go it alone away from the main ranch, unwashed and ragged, He did not return the friendly greetings called by Madigan and the others.

'We on Broken J land here?' Madigan asked.

'Mebbe.'

Madigan gestured to the horses taking the opportunity to graze. 'Bound for Hi-spade's.'

'So?'

'Just want to make sure we're headed in the right direction.'

'Keep goin' and you'll find out, won't you? One way or t'other.'

Madigan nodded. 'Yeah. Obliged for your help.'

'You stay clear of my camp!' Yeah – a man living like this soon became possessive of everything he used.

'Glad to,' Madigan told him.

They passed the camp on a bench, tucked back beside a spring, and Bobcat ventured down to fill the canteens. He came back spitting and holding his nose.

'Seen a vixen's lair cleaner'n this, right after she's whelped.'

By afternoon, they were in sight of the ranch. There was a neat house, though it was a simple oblong of logs and cedar shakes on the roof. But the fireplace was built of riverstones and as the river itself gleamed way, way over, Madigan figured it must be a luxury and someone must have lost a deal of sweat, hide and flesh hauling all those stones up here on a sled.

The barn was made of vertical clapboards, in fair repair, and the corrals were strong. Some muscular mountain-bred horses milled about, shrilling at sight and smell and sound of Madigan's herd.

A man appeared in the doorway of the house, holding an octagonal-barrelled Winchester, a '66 model, Madigan figured when sunlight flashed on the brass action. He left Bobcat and Cliff to watch the horses didn't rush the stream until they had cooled off some, lifted a hand and walked his mount across to the man.

'Name's Bronco Brennan – Captain Kerry Bodine sent me up here with these horses for you. That's if you're Hi-spade Billy Chandler.'

'You know damn well who I am, Madigan.'

The marshal tensed, thumbed back his hat and looked more closely. He swore under his breath.

'Norb Cantrell! Hell almighty, so this is where you ended up! We still got a dodger or two out on you, Norb.'

'You know where you can shove 'em.'

'Now, is that friendly?'

'I don't aim it to be. Damn you, Madigan! I've got me a good life up here, fine wife, nice little spread, make a livin' that wouldn't exactly suit royalty, I guess, but I'm happy. Or was till I seen you ridin' in.'

Madigan was silent for a time, watching Bobcat and Cliff drive the horses into a pasture. Hi-spade's gaze followed Madigan's. He was a medium-sized man but hard-faced, older than Madigan recalled, but then it had been a while.

'Just how long is it you've been up here in this neck of the woods, Norb?'

'Since you come in the front door of that hovel below the Rio while I went out the back window.'

Madigan arched his eyebrows. 'Nigh on six years. You must've gotten the money somewhere to set up here.'

'What d'you care? Where I got it weren't anywheres in your jurisdiction.'

'Down in *mañana* land, huh?'

'Built on it with a little gamblin'.'

'Heard stories about this high-stakes gambler who called himself Hi-spade, worked the riverboats for a spell, then disappeared.'

'Met a fine woman, half-breed.' This last was said belligerently, but almost immediately he added:

'Well, guess that makes no nevermind to you. You never did bother about the colour of anyone's skin, long as they obeyed the goddamn law!' He looked towards the cowboys again. Almost smiled. 'Deal?'

'What?'

'You're workin' under over – Bronco Brennan, you called yourself. Now I'll just bet my best Hereford cross against a cupful of panther piss that them fellers don't know who you really are.'

Madigan said nothing. Hi-spade's grin widened.

'Right, ain't I?'

'Could be, Norb. Thing is, it wouldn't really matter if they did know I'm a US marshal. They got no love for Kerry Bodine and they'd help me out if I asked 'em to.'

The rancher's face hardened. His grip tightened on the rifle.

'So it's Bodine you're after. Well, I got no love for him, neither. You gonna take me in, then?'

'Reckon not, Norb. If you're settled here. And your wife's a good enough cook to give us supper.'

Hi-spade answered right away, bristling a little.

'Ally's a fine cook. Supper'll be the best damn meal you've had in a coon's age, guaranteed. But, you mean what you said?'

'We've known each other long enough for you to recall I give my word, I keep it.'

'Yeah! You promised me you'd run me to ground!'

Madigan spread his hands. 'I have. Now, introduce me to your wife and let's eat. Then you can show me a short cut over the range to a place called Buckskin Ridge.'

'And. . . ?' Hi-spade wanted it all spelled out.

'And then it's *adios* and *muchas gracias.*'

Hi-spade gave a crooked smile and lowered the rifle. 'Just as well you didn't add *amigo* or I'd be really suspicious!'

Hi-spade was right: his wife was an excellent cook – and a good-looker, young, supple, shy, with big eyes and a smile hovering around a small mouth. She was several months pregnant, Madigan judged, and she offered them beds for the night. Bobcat and Cliff were willing but Madigan shook his head.

'Thanks all the same, ma'am. But I've got to get going.' He looked at the disappointed cowboys. 'You fellers stay if you like. I can pay you off right now – I'll take the other horses down to Buckskin Ridge and meet the train.'

They exchanged glances.

'Maybe you better have company,' Bobcat said and Hi-spade stiffened.

'If you think I'm gonna jump him in the dark. . . !'

'Back up there, pardner!' Bobcat drawled. 'No such thing meant. We ain't dumb, Bronco, and, by the by, Hi-spade here called you "Madigan" twice and you answered both times. An' you called him "Norb" and *he* answered. Look, we figure Cap's got somethin' goin' with Tex and Whip Weaver. Why else would he want three saddled hosses waitin' at the steepest grade on the Alamosa–Creede run? They're out to nail you after what you done to Tex and Whip and – well, we kinda like the idea of takin' care of an old feller like you.'

137

'Wait just a goddamn minute!' Madigan bristled and Bobcat grinned, but it was Cliff who said:

'He's sayin' you treated us good, Bronco, not like trash, which is how them rough-riders see us.'

'You don't owe me anything, boys.'

' 'Course not. We're just givin' you the pleasure of our company on a long, lonely ride. Besides, we want to see you tame down that damn piebald. He's throwed us too many times.'

And that's the way it was.

Hi-spade showed them a short cut through the ridges, deep down in dark timbered cuttings that overlooked some of the ranches down on the flats. Madigan suspected that these would be mighty handy trails for any man who wanted to throw a wide loop while collecting 'strays' that had wandered away from those cattle down on the flats . . . but he said nothing. He was convinced Hi-spade was a reformed character. Anyway, hell, Norb Cantrell had never been much on violence, just grabbed what money he could and made a run for it. Fact was, Madigan had unconsciously based his own cover of Bronco Brennan, the bank-robber, on Norb's mode of operation.

So, in a way, he owed Norb something and paid the debt by deciding to keep his mouth shut.

They topped out on the crest of a ridge and Hi-spade pointed towards the rising moon.

'Dead ahead. You can even see a glint of silver way over. That's the railroad track before it starts up the grade.' He hipped in saddle, studied Madigan a moment. 'You better watch Bodine. He surrounds himself with killers.'

'I've already tangled with the *Trio Courageous* and made 'em a duo. Utah's out of it now.'

Hi-spade pursed his lips, cocked his head on one side.

'Yeah. But you come up agin the woman yet?'

Madigan felt himself stiffen. 'You mean Lady Anne?'

'Lady Vixen! She ain't no Limey lady and you must know that. But she's a killer.'

There was a sudden sour taste in the back of Madigan's throat.

'A *killer*?'

'Yep. Seen her down in El Paso. First and only woman deputy town marshal there. She killed three men while I was there, shot the eyes clear out of one feller's head with them shiny little pistols. Wounded four or five others . . .'

'When the hell was this?'

'Aw, be eight, mebbe ten years ago.'

Madigan's body was cold from the inside out: something told him that Hi-spade was telling the truth.

'You gotta be mistaken, Norb!'

Stubbornly, Hi-spade shook his head. 'Nope. Seen it happen. Called herself Charity Fletcher then. Them little .22s of hers were poppin' like crackers at the Christmas dinner table. And she kept shootin' all the way down to the ground to make sure them fellers *stayed* down. Coldest thing I ever did see: her name mighta been "Charity" but she never showed none on the streets of El Paso.'

Madigan snapped his fingers. 'That was her *job*! El

Paso ten years ago was no Sunday-school, Norb. Not one even now. Clay Hardin was riding high, wide and handsome there at that time. Scum of the earth coming in day and night. Seems I did hear there was a lady badge-toter . . . she just had to be rougher and tougher was all.'

Hi-spade squinted. 'Just know what I seen. You be careful.' Then, hesitantly, he held out his hand. 'Thanks, Madigan.'

The marshal shook hands briefly. 'You treat that little gal well, Norb. I'll come back this way some time and I expect to see a few brats running around and hope they look like Ally instead of you.'

'Well, I ain't gonna name any of 'em after you, but I guess you'll be welcome.'

He dropped back and faded away into the night and the others drove the small bunch of horses down the ridge.

'You law of some kind?' asked Cliff after a while.

'Some kind.'

Cliff grunted and rode off swinging his rope as the piebald broke clear of the main bunch yet again.

'I don't want you boys involved in any shooting,' Madigan said to Bobcat.

'Hell, if there's gonna be *shootin'* I'm goin' home. Right after it's over!'

Madigan shook his head, smiling, glad of the back-up.

But that news about Lady Anne sure bothered him.

CHAPTER 12

BUCKSKIN RIDGE

The train was late. The loading of all the Wild West Show's gear took more time than expected and the depot agent at Del Norte proclaimed the six flatbed wagons too dangerous to be connected to the train: the stacked show-gear stowed on them was far too high to be safe.

Captain Bodine gave him an argument strengthened by a couple of double-eagles but the agent was adamant: he was responsible for the safety of this train and its passengers and freight. He pocketed the money anyway, but still made the fuming show-folk wait until an extra flatbed could be found.

Eventually all was to his satisfaction and the armoured express car was hitched on, followed by the caboose. And well after dark the train chugged and puffed and whistled its way out of Del Norte, iron wheels skidding against iron rails with the weight, showering sparks.

The three heavily armed guards in the express car

watched expressionlessly through the bars covering the high-set windows. Scoop vents on the roof brought cooling night air into the car but the men sweated just the same. They were independent of the rest of the train as far as cooking and coffee-making facilities were concerned, even the toilet, but they were still edgy: two were, anyway. Martin was more at ease than the others: he had had more experience than Hunnicutt and Jackson, although Hunnicutt was the one in charge. Martin didn't care about being passed over: he was due to retire after a couple more runs, anyway. He didn't aim to rock the boat and maybe make a dent in his pension.

Hunnicutt was good but he was a worrier and this one worried him to hell and back: nigh on a $100,000 in gold, if you could believe the men in the office – Hunnicutt had made sure the other two weren't shown the lading bill. If he was being given the responsibility, then he aimed to carry all of it. A petty ambitious type, was Cameron Hunnicutt, out for glory: *his*. Jackson – well, Jackson was tough, a gunman who liked to shoot. He was happy enough just riding along and gambling that he might get the chance to do just that.

Martin found himself a snug corner near the coal-oil stove and arranged mailsacks to sprawl on with a small pile of parcels for a footrest. Let the others stare out of the barred windows or the glass in the connecting door. There was nothing to see in the dark and whatever was there, Martin had seen it all before during his ten years with Wells Fargo.

He settled down with hands folded over his thickening waistline and was soon snoring, earning a scowl from Hunnicutt. Jackson cleaned and oiled his shotgun.

In the second special car that Bodine had hired for this run he and Lady Anne, Tyrell and Weaver ate their late supper. All had been ravenous, having worked through the earlier delay. When they had finished the meal and the attendant came to take away the plates, Bodine slipped him a silver dollar, smiled and said:

'Tell the conductor I want to see him, would you, friend?'

The man said he would and hurried out. Lady Anne looked quickly at the others and said:

'I'm turning in. And I don't expect to be woken up until I'm good and ready.'

'Of course, my dear,' Bodine told her easily and gestured to a small section that had been curtained off with heavy brown velvet bearing the railroad company's crest. 'You have your own private compartment. We wish you sweet dreams.'

She said: 'They'd better be!' and pulled the heavy drapes aside, stumbling as the train swayed and rocked so that she had to grab the corner post of the small bed beyond. She righted herself, drew the velvet across and sat down on the edge of the bed. She took out her nickel-plated pistols, checking the loads before placing them both beneath the silken pillow. The target rifle was in its scabbard, leaning beside the window that looked out on to dark, unseen countryside.

The men's voices were just a blur because of the heavy drapes and she lay back on the bed, still wearing her corduroy pants and tooled riding-boots. She unbuttoned the top two buttons of her dark-blue woollen shirt and locked her hands behind her head. After a while she closed her eyes, dozing, rocked by the train as it sped into the foothills on the approach to the steep grade of Buckskin Ridge.

The conductor wasn't sure he was doing the right thing, but a fifty-dollar gold piece salved his conscience as he unlocked the door leading to the small, swaying, clattering platform in the connecting, concertina-like tunnel between the special car and the express van. He did not have an access key to the express van door, of course, so he rapped hard on the barred window, cupping hands around his eyes as he tried to see into the dimly lit interior.

Behind him, a smiling Kerry Bodine urged Tyrell and Weaver on as they carried a wooden box, padlocked and obviously heavy, between them. They set it down on the moving platform at their feet, the noise of the rails and clashing couplings and rumble of the wheels mighty loud out here.

A face appeared at the barred window in the door and Bodine knew it was Hunnicutt. Hunnicutt frowned, opened the speaking grille on his side and snarled:

'You're not supposed to be on that platform, conductor. Nor are those passengers! Now go back into your car or you run the risk of being shot!'

The conductor had his ear close to the grille so he could hear above the noise, looked quickly at Bodine. The captain frowned, nodded, pointed a finger jerkily at the express van door.

'Ask!'

The conductor, middle-aged, silver-grey hair showing beneath his cap, spoke quickly before the guard could close the grille.

'This is Captain Kerry Bodine, of the Wild West Show.'

'Don't care if he's the goddamn president of the railroad, no one's s'posed to be on that platform! Now get off! That's my last warning!'

Bodine frowned and prodded the conductor, jerking his head at the window.

'Damn you, man! Gimme back my fifty dollars!'

The conductor licked his lips and held up a hand.

'Mr Hunnicutt! Listen. This railroad has been paid a lot of money by Captain Bodine and I've been instructed to give him whatever service he wants. Just give me a chance to speak, dammit! Now, he boarded this train and, as was his right, expected things to go smoothly and on time. But, what with delays caused by the depot agent, the banks had closed long before we got things sorted out. So Captain Bodine wasn't able to deposit quite a large sum of money that was paid to him for sale of his troupe of horses and also the takings from his last show. What he wants to know is, can he put that money in your safe-keeping in the express car until we reach Alamosa? Quite a reasonable request, as I think you'll agree.'

'No, I don't!' shouted Hunnicutt. 'I'm not supposed to open this door before we pull into the Alamosa depot, except in an emergency.'

Bodine shouldered up to the door and pushed the conductor away from the grille.

'What the hell d'you think this is? This *is* an emergency, sir! I have the better part of thirty thousand dollars in that box my men are carrying and I'm damned if I'm going to have it sitting under my bed or anywhere else on this train when there's plenty of room in the express car! I'll have you know also, that your company president, Charles Benson, is a personal friend of mine.'

'That don't cut no ice with me, mister!' Hunnicutt said, but there was just a vague note of uncertainty in his tone. 'I've got my orders.'

'And you're to be commended for carrying them out to the letter,' Bodine said. 'Obedience is a marvellous thing, but so is initiative. You have a position of responsibilty which I do not envy, but if I have to send a wire to Chuck Benson to the effect that my cash-box was stolen or even that someone *attempted* to steal it, because it had to be kept in a vulnerable position, due to you refusing me space to store it safely in an express car that is *ninety per cent* unused space, then I see your career going right out of the window. I'll give you five minutes to think about it . . .'

Hunnicutt didn't like it, but he was a man on the verge of making a 'good' marriage and the success of that wonderful event depended in great part on his career prospects being far more than average. As Bodine said, initiative – the right *kind* of initiative – was important and could well carry the day.

He bit his bottom lip, and eventually, under the silent stare of Jackson and accompanied by Martin's snores, he took the big brass door-key and inserted it in the lock. He hesitated a moment longer, turned it and swung open the door.

'Bring in your cash-box – and be quick about it!'

The conductor was trying to stand aside to let Bodine and his men pass but there wasn't enough room on the swaying platform. Bodine pushed him in ahead of him impatiently, stepped after him and motioned to Tyrell and Weaver to carry in the heavy box.

Jackson, caught off-guard, hurriedly assembled his shotgun, poked Martin hard in the ribs, then saw there was no real hurry: Hunnicutt was already covering the visitors with his cocked pistol.

The head guard noted straight away that neither Tyrell nor Weaver wore sixguns and he relaxed a little. Then he jerked his gun barrel at the box, which seemed to be causing the two men some strain to hold.

'Set down the box. You . . .' He indicated Weaver. 'Stand over there beside the captain.' He set his gaze on Tyrell then. 'Kneel down and open that box.'

Tyrell looked up at Bodine who nodded jerkily. 'Do as he asks, Tex. Show him how much money we have in there.' Bodine held out a key to Tyrell who took it, unlocked the padlock, slid it from the hasp and lifted the lid. It could not go all the way back because a leather strap on the inside allowed it only to open just far enough past the vertical and to remain in that position.

Tyrell reached to turn the box around. 'See? All stacked neatly and . . .'

The express van shook to the roar of a sawn-off shotgun, splinters exploding as the charge of buck-shot shattered the lid of the cash-box before slamming into Hunnicutt's chest. It lifted him clear off

the floor and flung him back so that his bloody, life-
less body fell across the legs of Martin who was just
now struggling to get out of the mailbag bed. Jackson
swore and brought his gun up, snapping it closed on
a shell as he lurched to his feet.

The train swayed as it gathered speed and made its
run at the first steep rise of Buckskin Ridge. Jackson
fell back, his shotgun blasting a hole in the roof.
Weaver shoulder-rolled and came up with a Colt that
he had had rammed into his belt under his jacket.
Jackson wrenched the gun towards him, seeing him as
the immediate danger. Weaver triggered just as Tyrell
fired the second barrel of the shortened shotgun that
had been lying inside the otherwise empty box.

Jackson didn't have a chance and went down in a
bath of blood. Before he hit the floor, the killers' guns
were seeking Martin. Tyrell dropped the now empty
shotgun and grabbed his own Colt from inside his shirt.

Martin finally kicked free of Hunnicutt's broken
body, fired his rifle across the corpse, dived behind a
pile of mailbags. Bullets ripped into the sacks and
torn letters erupted from the rents in the canvas like
a small snowstorm. Martin rolled on to his back, kicking mailbags in the direction of the killers, confusing
their aim. He burrowed down, roared to his feet,
mailbags flying in all directions. The rifle butt was
braced into his hip as he worked lever and trigger,
filling the van with a deadly swarm of hot lead.

Captain Bodine dived for the floor but not before
he experienced a stinging, burning pain across the
lower part of his arm. The conductor came unfrozen
at last and ran for the door. Bodine pulled out a

derringer and gave the man both barrels, one after the other. The conductor slumped in the connecting concertina, groaning and bleeding.

By that time Martin was dead, shot five times by Tyrell and Weaver. He was swaying on his knees, bloody and already departed from this world. Weaver reached out languidly with one finger and flicked his shoulder, as though he was flicking a fly off the edge of a plate. Martin collapsed.

'Bastard – winged me,' Tyrell gasped and they saw him holding his side low down, a little blood trickling through his fingers.

'Bad?' asked Bodine, dabbing at a facial scratch, but there wasn't a lot of interest in the question: he was looking at the red-painted safe with the oval brass badge on it bearing the Wells Fargo name.

'Nah. Just a gouge,' Tyrell said but no one was listening.

Weaver was probing amongst the bloody cloth and ragged flesh of Hunnicutt's mid-section, coming up at last with the man's ring of keys.

'It'll be one of these,' he said. He made as though to toss them towards Bodine, who held up both hands and stepped back.

'I don't want blood all over me. Open it up and stack the gold in that box. Pity about the lid, but it'll do to carry it back to the car.'

'I hope Brennan and the others are waiting!' growled Tyrell. 'I still owe that son of a bitch!'

Bodine grinned as Weaver found the right key and the safe opened. Despite the dim lamplight, he squinted his eyes against the bright flash of yellow.

'Boys – what you smell ain't blood and gunsmoke: it's the easy life! Just waiting for us to go and enjoy it!'

'Where the hell's the train?' griped Cliff, standing restlessly atop a lichen-scarred boulder half-way up Buckskin Ridge. 'It's late as hell!'

Bobcat and Madigan knew that. The marshal had been champing at the bit when there had been no sign of the train but no one would know it to look at him. In the moonlight he appeared relaxed and patient. They were all three wearing the slickers provided by Captain Bodine. Instead of the usual drab dark brown, this time they were shiny light grey.

'Just hope there's no Yankees on board who might mistake you for Johnny Rebs!' Bodine had quipped.

But Madigan wasn't so sure there was anything to joke about. Light grey under the light of a waxing moon, against the dark backdrop of heavy timber and boulders on Buckskin Ridge could make a fine target.

'There!' Bobcat said suddenly, standing beside Cliff and pointing. 'She's comin'!'

Madigan climbed to his feet. He could see the shower of sparks and the glow of the fire in the engineer's cab as the train rocked along the straight before the run-up to the grade. He had abandoned his plan of riding downtrack to get aboard before the loco reached the grade. When there had been no sign of the train, even out along the wide sweep of the rails on the approach to the Ridge, he figured it had been delayed. He had ridden down and checked the rails, finding several yards covered in a trickling layer of dew and some dead leaves. If the train had

already passed it would have swept the track clear of
dew and debris and they wouldn't have had time to
settle back again.

So he had decided to wait half-way up the steep
grade where he could get a view of the approaches and
see the train when it was coming across to the ridge.

'OK, fellers, let's get mounted and ride down.'

They stared at him. Bobcat spoke.

'Man, you see how fast that train's a-comin? It's
gettin' a run-on so it can hit the grade and not lose
so much speed climbin' it.'

'We'll bust a leg – or our necks – we try to swing
aboard at that speed, Bronco,' Cliff added.

Madigan hesitated: the damn robbery had probably
taken place by now, anyway. His timing had been
wrong. He hadn't thought about a delay in the train's
arrival at Buckskin Ridge. And the boys were right:
trying to jump on board at the speed that train was
going would more than likely end in disaster all round.

He climbed into the saddle of the piebald which
snorted and moved restlessly but it knew his touch
now and he stroked that left ear and spoke quietly,
settling it. The others mounted, gathered the reins of
the three getaway mounts, and Madigan led the way
down and across the slope.

The train was already slowing as it hit the first
steep rise. The rapid thundering of hot air punching
out of the smokestack slowed perceptibly and the
labouring began as the loco hauled its load around
the first of the curves.

The deal had been for Madigan and the others to
be waiting in the region of those lichen-scarred

rocks but he led the way across the slope, aiming to try to board lower down. Not that he was supposed to climb on board at all, but he had to take charge now, not follow Bodine's orders: that way could lead to all their deaths. He was going to play this by *his* rules: it was their only chance of coming out alive.

There was the signal. They must have been spotted already. Damn these light slickers! He ought to have abandoned them! Too late now! A man was leaning out from the swaying platform between the special car and the crew's car ahead, waving a white neckerchief.

'Spread out,' Madigan ordered quietly, 'and keep your hands on your guns.'

'You call it, Bronco!' Bobcat said and they reined aside, he and Cliff taking two horses apiece. Three were apparently for the men themselves and the fourth, most likely, for whatever loot they had managed to grab.

Madigan's lips tightened: that meant dead men on board and . . . Something burned across his neck and he went sideways out of the saddle, wrenching the reins involuntarily as he did so. It yanked the piebald's head around violently, a position it hated, and it lunged away with an angry snort. Madigan was unprepared for the snaking twist of the big body, slipped out of his natural fall – and felt his left boot twist and catch in the stirrup.

Even as he jarred against the ground and the piebald took off with a bunching of muscles, he knew he was in for a hell-ride, bouncing across this rocky slope until his brains were smashed out. He tried to sit up and reach the stirrup so he could take the strain off, get some slack and twist his boot free. No hope.

The piebald was away and loving the freedom of the run.

Madigan looked around for Cliff and Bobcat. He was in time to see Cliff stand straight in his stirrups, put up a hand as if to brush at his face, and then the man toppled out of the saddle, crashing to the ground, rolling a little way before becoming still.

Bouncing, gritting his teeth, Madigan searched for Bobcat. The man's horse had veered to one side and Bobcat was hanging over the saddle, his light grey slicker now stained with something dark. It seemed to be shredded – as if from a hail of bullets.

But he hadn't heard a sound! Nothing but the train and it wasn't loud enough to drown a gunshot, not this close.

Bobcat fell, flopped limply and lay still. And then Madigan had his hands full, bouncing and twisting as the piebald raced across the ridge, going downhill as that was easier.

He still had his sixgun in his hand as he had when he had first approached the train. He started to cock the hammer but stopped almost immediately. Shooting the bolting horse was a last resort. He had seen men do it time and again – and time and again the horse had fallen on top of them, causing horrific injuries, sometimes agonizing death. But he had to do something.

There was blood wetting his neck and shirt collar. The slicker was shredded from the drag and in moments he was able to struggle free of it. Hoofs thudded down beside him, hurling stones and dirt and grass into his face. He was spitting out what he could but still chewed on plenty of grit.His senses were spinning, his brain loose in his skull, thudding with each hoof smashing into the ground inches away. One shoe grazed his shoulder and the pain almost made him lose his grip on the gun. His hat was gone and his head banged off a small tuft of grass, gashing one ear. *Hell, that had been only grass! What if it had been a rock. . . ?*

Desperate measures were called for and he started to cock the gun hammer again, fighting to control his twisting body. A hoof shot clumps of dirt into his face. His nose was bleeding now, and in desperation he swung his gun hand. The barrel connected with the left foreleg just below the knee and he felt the piebald falter.

Instantly, he knew what had happened. He hadn't hurt the animal so much as triggered an instinctive reaction. When he had been training the horse he had used the shin-tapper where the end of the chain hit against the left foreleg if the horse tried to run or even move fast, forcing it to keep to a slow, hobbled pace.

The gun barrel striking must have felt just like the chain and the piebald had instinctively slowed. Madigan struck out again. And again. The horse snorted angrily, tossed its head, but its pace slowed noticeably and after a few more jarring cracks with the revolver it slowed to walking pace and eventually halted, panting loudly, its sweat dripping into Madigan's taut, blood-streaked face.

In seconds he had twisted his boot free of the stirrup. Shakily he climbed into the saddle and set the piebald up-slope, alongside the slow-moving train. There was no sign of Bodine or any of his men. The sons of bitches had done their dirty work, killed Bobcat and Cliff and made their try for Madigan. They would figure him as dead, too, being dragged away like that by the piebald.

The marshal had already figured things out: he was mad at himself for not seeing it before. All along, he had felt it was a trap, but he couldn't see at first why they would go to all that trouble if they only wanted him and the others dead. That could have been managed anywhere, long ago.

But Bodine was more cunning than that. Three dead men found beside the track with what were obviously saddled getaway mounts. Any lawman would figure they were cut down as they tried to escape. The loot? Maybe there had been a fourth man and he had gotten away with it. . . .

Either way, he would not figure that the killers were still on board – and the loot as well. The train would be the last place anyone would expect men who had just robbed the express car to try to hide out.

Madigan not merely suspected, he *knew*! His hunches were working overtime and now he swung the protesting piebald in close enough to grab a handrail on the side of the crew's car, past the windows, close to the joining platform that led to Bodine's special car.

The motion of the train, as well as the change in his speed, leaping from a running horse on to the slow train, flung Madigan's body hard against the side of the car. He grunted as breath burst from him, fought to swing back around so he could grab the rail with both hands. His boots were dangling, banging against the edge of the car, just above the whirling wheels. If he fell, he would be dog-meat.

He was just swinging his boots on to the edge of the heaving platform when the door of the special car opened and Tex Tyrell came out, clutching his sawn-off shotgun. Something had aroused his suspicions, or he may even have seen Madigan leave the racing piebald which had dropped way back now down the slope. Tyrell bared his teeth in savage pleasure at coming face to face with the man he hated most on this earth.

'Give my regards to Utah when you get to hell, Brennan!'

The shotgun lifted, both hammers back, and Madigan swung by one hand, let go and triggered as he fell, clawing at the wrought-iron railing that ran around the platform for passengers to grip when boarding or alighting or just to stand there and admire the view. His boots found the step as the shotgun roared and something bit savagely into his face.

It was a long splinter. From the side of the car. One at least of his bullets had found Tyrell before the man pulled the trigger, and now Madigan flung his body on to the platform, rolled and fired twice more. Tex Tyrell staggered in a strange little death-dance, poised a moment and then his body struck Madigan's as it hurtled from the train.

The shotgun had stirred the crew in their car, and someone was trying to open the door to the platform. But Madigan concentrated on the special car, got his legs under him and went in, shoulder-rolling, glimpsing Whip Weaver and the captain coming fast down the passage leading to the door, saw a movement behind them as some brown drapes were eased aside and Lady Anne appeared, rifle in hand.

He had no more time to notice her, just yelled for her to 'Get the hell down!' and then the car was full of thunder as Bodine and Weaver fired at his rolling body. He flung himself left, kicked off a seat and his body arced across to the other side of the car, bullets ripping the floorboards all round him.

He brought up close against the wall on his side, put a bullet through the middle of Weaver's face, felt the wind of a slug from Bodine's pistol, and emptied his gun into the captain.

Kerry Bodine's body hit the floor hard and then something burned across Madigan's left arm and he heard a dull crack. Looking up he saw that Lady Anne had triggered her rifle at him and was working the lever to do it again.

He rolled across Weaver's body, snatched up the man's sixgun and fired as she triggered a second time. He didn't see where her bullet went but his struck sparks from her rifle's breech and she gave a small cry as the weapon was hurled across the room. She backed up into the small compartment, dragging the drapes closed.

Madigan could see someone coming across the platform from the crew's car, kicked the door closed and heard it click. Fists hammered on the wood but he ignored them, rolled under the drapes in time to see her wrenching her two target pistols from under the pillow. He fired into the pillow, filling the compartment with a storm of down feathers. Instinctively, she struck at them as they went into her hair and eyes and face and he stood and smashed both pistols from her small hands with his smoking gun barrel.

She twisted towards him, eyes narrowed, panting, staring malevolently. He glanced at the small-calibre rifle.

'So that's why I never heard the shots that killed Cliff and Bobcat! Ought to've figured it out long before this. By hell, I *must* be getting old! Bodine wasn't the brains behind this. It was you! One-time Lady Deputy of El Paso.'

She showed surprise at that. 'Who told you?'

'Hi-spade Billy. Saw you in El Paso about ten years ago. Said you shot a man's eyes out of his head.'

Her lip curled. 'The bastard spied on me while I was bathing. Well, who *are* you? I know you're some kind of lawman. I suspected it soon after you arrived. I warned Bodine, but like all you men, he just laughed it off. "Woman's notion", he called it.'

'Name's Madigan – Federal Marshal.'

'I knew we should never have stolen army payrolls but it was really too good a chance to pass up. Bodine still had contacts in the army. We were too greedy, I guess.'

'Well, whatever your motives, they've landed you on the gallows.'

She laughed briefly. 'You can't prove a thing!'

'Maybe not. But I'd still like to know *why* you got into this.'

She smiled, with a devilish slant to her eyes.

'Why? It was nothing too complicated, what you men would call a "woman's thing", I suppose. My husband was a bastard, lost no opportunity to put me down, even said I wasn't a real woman because I could-n't have children.' The lip curled and there was a glint of remembered vicious pleasure in her eyes. 'So I told him if that was the case, there was no point in him continuing with what he saw as his conjugal rights.'

She paused, waiting for Madigan's comment but he had none to make.

'So – he took to drinking and beating me. The one thing I could do well, and even he admitted this, was shoot a gun and hit what I aimed at. So, one day I aimed at him.'

'Killed him?'

'He deserved to die. After that, killing seemed to come easy. But the El Paso town council didn't like me killing those men, said what happened was that I was really afraid and I'd acted in panic; didn't think, just shot to kill so as to get myself out of danger.'

'And you didn't?'

The eyes narrowed. ' I – shot – to – kill because I wanted to! It was just like killing my louse of a husband over and over again and I liked that. Then the council discharged me, said a sheriff's deputy was no job for a woman, anyway! I knew Bodine because he used to deal in guns and whiskey with my husband. He needed a shooting act and I was the best around – still am. He eventually told me he had an idea that would make us all rich but he couldn't plan things. That was where I came in.' Her face hardened. 'We could've gotten away with it a lot longer except for you, Madigan!'

He made a small, mocking bow.

'Glad you realize this is the end of the line, my lady.'

'You fool! D'you think any jury would hang me?'

As soon as she spoke, he knew she was right. With her looks and the 'English' accent, a fluttering of those long, curling eyelashes and a few tears in appropriate places and he'd be lucky if the jury didn't hang *him*!

He would never get them to believe this beautiful woman had masterminded those robberies and ruthless killings. But *he* knew.

And that was more than enough for Bronco Madigan.

As he stood there, cocked pistol trained on her, she smiled mockingly and quite confidently.

'All for nothing, Madigan?'

'Maybe we won't need a jury.'

That startled her and momentarily there was desperation and possibly a touch of fear in those eyes. Then she twisted her mouth contemptuously and tore open her shirt front, held it wide so he could see her perfect white breasts with the erecting pink nipples against the darker circles of the aureoles.

'Could you destroy this, Madigan?' she sneered.

He stared back, silent for a long moment, and she smiled triumphantly just as he said:

'Easy.'

And pulled the trigger.